D1485385

Mary-Mary

"— such a success on the stall —"

Mary-Mary

written and illustrated by

JOAN G. ROBINSON

HOT
KEY
BOOKS

Published in Great Britain in 2013 by Hot Key Books
Northburgh House, 10 Northburgh Street, London EC1V 0AT

Mary-Mary first published by George G. Harrap & Co. Ltd in 1957

More Mary-Mary first published by George G. Harrap & Co. Ltd in 1958

A CIP catalogue record for this book is available from the British Library.

ISBN: 978-1-4714-0205-0

1

This book is typeset in 11pt Sabon using Atomik ePublisher

Printed and bound by Clays Ltd, St Ives Plc

FSC

Hot Key Books supports the Forest Stewardship Council (FSC),
the leading international forest certification organisation, and is committed to
printing only on Greenpeace-approved FSC-certified paper.

www.hotkeybooks.com

Hot Key Books is part of the Bonnier Publishing Group
www.bonnierpublishing.com

JF

For SUSANNA

Contents

1

Mary-Mary Goes Visiting

ONCE upon a time there was a little girl called Mary-Mary.

She was the youngest of five, and all her brothers and sisters were very big and clever, and knew all about everything. Mary-Mary didn't know much about anything; so all her big brothers and sisters, who were called Miriam, Martyn, Mervyn, and Meg, used to say to her, "Don't do it like that, Mary-Mary. Do it like this!" or "Don't go that way, Mary-Mary. Come this way!"

Then Mary-Mary would say, "No. I shall do it my own way," and, "No. I am going the other way."

And that, of course, is why she was called Mary-Mary instead of just Mary, which was her real name.

One day Mary-Mary started coming downstairs backwards, pulling a box of bricks behind her.

Miriam, Martyn, Mervyn, and Meg were all standing together in the hall, and when they heard Mary-Mary coming

"Don't come down backward, Mary-Mary. You'll fall down!"

bumpety-bump down the stairs backwards they all started shouting at her at once:

"Don't come down backwards, Mary-Mary. You'll fall down!"

Mary-Mary fell down. And all the bricks came after her.

"There!" said Miriam. "We said you'd fall down."

"There!" said Martyn. "We knew you would."

"There!" said Mervyn. "Just as we said."

"There!" said Meg. "What did we tell you?"

"You told me to fall down," said Mary-Mary, "and I think it was very silly of you."

She sat on the bottom stair and looked to see which of

her legs was broken. Neither of them was, so she picked up her box of bricks and sat them in her lap. She wasn't really hurt, only surprised.

Mother ran out of the kitchen.

"What was that bump?" she said.

"My bricks fell down and I'm nursing them better," said Mary-Mary.

All the others started talking to Mother at once. They were all wanting to do different things.

"Can I go round to Barbara's house?" said Miriam. "She wants to show me the new kitten."

"Can I go fishing with Billy?" said Martyn. "He's got a new fishing-line, and I can use his old one."

"Can I go and play with Bob?" said Mervyn. "He's got a new electric train."

Mother put her hands over her ears and said, "Please, please, don't all talk at once. Yes, Miriam, you can go to Barbara's. But be back in time for tea. Yes, Martyn, you can go fishing with Billy. But do be careful. Yes, Mervyn, you can go and play with Bob. But don't break his new train. Yes, Meg—what do you want?"

"Can I go shopping with Bunty?" said Meg. "She wants me to help her choose a present."

"Oh, yes," said Mother. "That will be nice for you, especially as all the others have been asked out too—all except Mary-Mary, of course."

"Why 'except me, of course'?" said Mary-Mary. "Why doesn't anyone ask me out?"

"Oh, but they do," said Mother. "You and I quite often

get asked out, don't we?"

"By myself, I mean," said Mary-Mary.

"Don't be silly," said Miriam.

"You're not old enough," said Martyn.

"You couldn't go alone," said Mervyn.

"You're too little," said Meg.

Then they all said, "Never mind, Mary-Mary," together, and went off to get ready.

Mary-Mary dragged her box of bricks out into the garden, talking to herself loudly all the way.

"When I'm a lady," she said, "I shall have lots and lots of children, but they'll all be exactly the same age. I won't have even one a little bit older than the others."

She began building a little house out of bricks for Moppet, her pet mouse.

Moppet was a toy mouse, with a key to wind him up, but he looked very real and was quite good for frightening people with if they didn't already know him.

Mary-Mary wrapped him in her handkerchief and put him down to sleep inside the little brick house.

"There you are, my pet," she said. "What you would do without me to look after you I just don't know. Now go to sleep, and when you're bigger I may let you go out visiting all by yourself."

Then she dragged the brick box close to the garden wall and climbed up on to it so that she could see over the other side.

Miriam, Martyn, Mervyn, and Meg were all tall enough to see over the wall into the next-door garden if they stood on tiptoe, but Mary-Mary couldn't. She was too little.

Just then Miriam came running out on her way to Barbara's house.

"Good-bye, Mary-Mary," she said. "Don't look over the wall. It's rude."

"Good-bye," said Mary-Mary. But she stayed where she was. Then Martyn came running out on his way to go fishing with Billy.

"Good-bye, Mary-Mary," he said. "Don't stare over the wall."

"Good-bye," said Mary-Mary, still standing on the box.

Then Mervyn ran out on his way to play with Bob.

"Good-bye, Mary-Mary," he said. "You'd better get down off that box."

"Good-bye," said Mary-Mary. But she still stayed where she was.

Then Meg ran out on her way to go shopping with Beauty.

"Good-bye, Mary-Mary," she said. "Don't stand on that box. And don't stare over the wall. It's rude. Anyway, you'll fall."

Mary-Mary fell, and by the time she had picked herself up again Meg had gone.

"Bother that girl," said Mary-Mary. "She's always making me fall down."

She peeped into the little brick house. Moppet's beady black eye was showing over the top of the handkerchief blanket. Mary-Mary brought him out, unwrapped him, and put him on top of the wall. Then she kicked down the little brick house and shouted in Moppet's voice, "Don't kick

The hat was just below her on the other side

the house down. It's rude." After that she walked once round the garden, then came back to Moppet, who was still sitting on the wall where she had left him.

"Moppet," said Mary-Mary sweetly, "you mustn't stare over the wall. It's rude. Anyway, you'll fall."

Then, quite by mistake, she gave him a little push with her hand, and he fell over the other side of the wall into the next-door garden.

Mary-Mary climbed up on the brick box and looked over the wall. But she couldn't see Moppet. He had fallen into the flower-bed and was too far down for her to see.

"Alas, poor Moppet," said Mary-Mary, and she got down and began walking round and round the garden, wondering how she was going to get him back again.

In a minute she heard the sound of a door opening, and then of footsteps in the next-door garden. Soon she saw the top of a large straw hat moving along behind the wall.

She climbed up on the box again. The large straw hat was just below her on the other side.

Mary-Mary made a little humming noise. The hat looked up, and there was a lady's face underneath it.

"Hallo," said the lady under the hat.

"Hallo," said Mary-Mary.

"How big you are!" said the lady. "Fancy being able to see over the top of the wall!"

"Yes," said Mary-Mary, "I am quite big." She thought for a minute and then she said, "But I'm not quite as big as this really. I'm standing on a box."

"Oh, I see," said the lady. "And what is your name?"

"I'm Mary-Mary. Who are you?"

"I'm Miss Summers. I'm your new neighbour. I've only been living here a few weeks."

"I've been living here for years and years," said Mary-Mary, "so I suppose I'm your old neighbour. Just now I'm looking for my mouse."

Then she told Miss Summers how Moppet had fallen over the wall.

Miss Summers looked all along the flower-bed, but she couldn't see Moppet.

"He must be somewhere," she said. "Perhaps one of your big brothers and sisters would like to come over and see if they can find him?"

"They are all out," said Mary-Mary. And she told Miss Summers all about how Miriam had gone to Barbara's house and Martyn had gone fishing with Billy and Mervyn had gone to play with Bob and Meg had gone shopping with Bunty, and how she had to stay at home until she was big enough to be asked out by herself.

"Well, then," said Miss Summers, "would you like to come? I wonder if I could lift you over the wall."

"If you would like me to come as a proper visitor I would come round to the front door," said Mary-Mary.

Miss Summers thought that would be a good idea.

"Yes, do come as a proper visitor," she said.

So Mary-Mary ran indoors, and along the passage to the front door. The front-door handle was rather high, but she could easily reach it if she jumped.

Mary-Mary held on to the net curtain that hung over the glass part of the door, and jumped. Something snapped, and the curtain fell to the floor.

Mary-Mary picked it up, put it round her shoulders, and looked in the hall mirror. She nodded at herself and said, "Good afternoon. I believe you are expecting me?" Then she went out, shut the door behind her, and walked slowly and politely round to the front of the next-door house.

Miss Summers opened the door at once.

"Good afternoon," said Mary-Mary. "I believe you are expecting me?"

"Oh, yes," said Miss Summers. "Good afternoon. Do come in. How nice of you to come."

"That's right," said Mary-Mary. "I'm glad you knew what I meant about being a proper visitor."

They went in. It was a very grown-up house with no toys anywhere, but there was a cuckoo clock in the hall and a

"Good afternoon. I believe you are expecting me?"

rocking-chair in the sitting-room, and in the kitchen, when they looked inside the door, Mary-Mary saw a plate of little pink cakes on the table.

"Those look pretty," she said.

"Yes," said Miss Summers. "I've just finished making them. We will have them for tea."

When Mary-Mary had rocked in the rocking-chair, played the piano, and seen the cuckoo come out twice, she went out into the garden, and there she found Moppet standing on his head under a hollyhock.

Miss Summers brought out two deck-chairs and a little table, and put them in the middle of the lawn.

"We will have tea out here, as it's so nice and sunny," she said. And she found a real lady's sunshade (which she didn't need herself, because she had her large straw hat),

9

— smiled secretly to herself and closed her eyes

and lent it to Mary-Mary. Then she went indoors to put the kettle on.

Mary-Mary sat in the long deck-chair, with the net curtain round her shoulders and the real lady's sunshade over her head, and felt like a very proper visitor.

When Miriam and Martyn and Mervyn and Meg came home they couldn't see Mary-Mary anywhere. They looked all over the house and all round the garden, but she was nowhere to be seen. Then they saw her brick box still standing by the wall.

"She couldn't have gone over, could she?" said Miriam.

"Oh, no," said Martyn, "she's not big enough."

"She wouldn't dare," said Mervyn. "It's too high."

"Let's just look and make sure," said Meg.

So they all stood in a row on tiptoe and looked over the wall into the next-door garden. And there what should they

"Whatever are you doing there?"

see but Mary-Mary sitting in a deck-chair with a little table by her side and a sunshade over her head!

"Mary-Mary!" they all said together. "Whatever are you doing there?"

Mary-Mary smiled secretly to herself and closed her eyes. It was very pleasant to be sitting in the sun like a grown-up lady.

Miriam and Martyn and Mervyn and Meg all started whispering together on the other side of the wall.

"Oh, isn't she naughty!"

"She's got over the wall."

"She's sitting in the next-door garden."

"Just as if she belonged there."

There was more whispering and rustling, and then the four heads appeared over the top of the wall again.

"Come back at once, Mary-Mary," said Miriam.

"Or we'll tell Mother," said Martyn.

"Someone might see you," said Mervyn.

"Hurry," said Meg.

Mary-Mary turned round slowly and smiled at them all

like a very beautiful lady.

"You mustn't look over the wall," she said. "It's rude."

Just then Miss Summers came out of the house carrying a tea-tray with two cups and saucers and the plateful of little pink cakes.

Miriam and Martyn and Mervyn and Meg all bobbed down behind the wall when they saw her coming, but Mary-Mary could hear them whispering together.

"Perhaps she was invited."

"She couldn't have been!"

"I wonder if Mother knows."

"I can't believe it."

When Miss Summers had put the tray down on the table Mary-Mary said, "Did you see a row of children with rather dirty faces looking over the wall just now?"

Miss Summers smiled.

"Yes, I thought I did," she said. "Were they your brothers and sisters?"

"I'm afraid so," said Mary-Mary. "They shouldn't have stared over the wall like that. I'm always telling them not to. But I'm sure they didn't mean to be so rude."

"Oh, I'm sure they didn't," said Miss Summers. "Now, do help yourself to a pink cake, won't you? Take two, as they're so small."

So Mary-Mary went visiting by herself after all, and that is the end of the story.

2

Mary-Mary Earns Some Money

ONE day Mary-Mary saw all her big brothers and sisters coming out of the kitchen looking very busy and important. Miriam had a bucket of water and a scrubbing-brush, Martyn had a broom, Mervyn had a set of shoe-brushes, and Meg had a packet of soap powder.

"What are you all going to do?" said Mary-Mary.

"Don't worry us now," said Miriam.

"We're busy," said Martyn.

"We're going to do some work," said Mervyn.

"And earn some money," said Meg.

Mary-Mary looked at the bucket of water, the packet of soap powder, and all the different kinds of brushes, and thought they looked interesting.

"I'll come too," she said.

But all the others turned round together and said, "Oh, no, Mary-Mary—not you! Now do go away."

So, of course, Mary-Mary followed them.

— so, of course, Mary-Mary followed them

Miriam went to the back-door step and began scrubbing it. Mary-Mary watched her and thought it looked rather fun to dip the brush in the bucket like that and slosh water all over the step.

"Are you going to get money for doing that?" she asked, rather surprised.

"Yes," said Miriam. "Threepence. When you're as big as me you'll be able to earn threepence too."

"I'll do it now," said Mary-Mary, reaching for the brush.

"Oh, no, you won't," said Miriam. "You'll upset the bucket."

Mary-Mary stepped backwards and sat in the bucket by mistake. It upset.

"Now look what you've done," said Miriam.

"I don't need to look," said Mary-Mary. "I can feel it. That water was very wet."

Miriam went off to fill the bucket with more water, and Mary-Mary, with her skirt all wet and dripping, went away to see what the others were doing.

Martyn was sweeping up the mess round the dustbins.

"Will you get threepence for doing that?" asked Mary-Mary.

"Yes," said Martyn; "so can you when you're as big as me."

"I'll start now," said Mary-Mary, reaching for the broom.

"No, you're not big enough," said Martyn. "You'd make yourself dirty."

Mary-Mary stepped backwards and tripped over a pile of dust and tea-leaves. It flew up all round her, and as she was wet it stuck to her in quite a lot of places.

"I seem to have got rather dirty," she said.

"I knew you would," said Martyn, and he started sweeping it up all over again.

So Mary-Mary, with her skirt all wet and dripping, and covered with dust and tea-leaves, went away to see what the others were doing.

Mervyn was kneeling on the garden step polishing shoes. Mary-Mary stood and watched for a while. Two tins of polish lay open on the step, one very black and the other shiny brown. Mervyn dipped one brush into the polish and put it on the shoes, then he rubbed them with another brush and polished them with a soft cloth until they shone.

"Do you like doing that?" asked Mary-Mary.

"Not much," said Mervyn, "but I'll get threepence for it."

Mary-Mary knelt down on the step beside him.

"Now I'll do some," she said.

"No, you won't," said Mervyn. "You'll only get covered

"Are you going to get money for doing that?"

in polish. Get up, now."

Mary-Mary got up, and the two tins of polish were stuck to her knees. She hadn't looked where she was kneeling, and the very black one was stuck to her right knee, and the shiny brown one was stuck to her left knee. She took them off quickly before Mervyn noticed. He was polishing hard.

"When you're as big as me you'll be able to earn threepence, too," he said. "Now do go away. You'll only get covered in polish."

Mary-Mary looked at her knees.

"I am already," she said, and rubbed some of it off on to her hands.

So Mary-Mary, with her skirt all wet and dripping, covered with dust and tea-leaves, and with shoe-polish on her hands and knees, went away to see what Meg was doing.

Meg was in the garden washing her dolls' blankets in a bowl.

"Why are you doing that?" said Mary-Mary.

"They were very dirty," said Meg, "and if I wash all the dolls' clothes as well I'm going to get threepence."

Mary-Mary picked up the packet of soap powder.

"I'll do some washing too," she said. "I'd like to earn threepence."

"You can't," said Meg. "You're too little. Wait till you're as big as me and then you can. Put down that packet—you'll spill it."

But Mary-Mary held the packet high above her head and wouldn't put it down.

"You're spilling it!" shouted Meg. "You've got it upside down. It's running all over your hair."

Mary-Mary put it down again.

"I wondered what was tickling my head," she said.

"Go away now," said Meg.

"No," said Mary-Mary, and stayed where she was.

"Oh, well, then—stay if you must," said Meg.

"No, I won't," said Mary-Mary. "I'm going away."

So Mary-Mary, with her skirt all wet and dripping, covered with dust and tea-leaves, with shoe-polish on her hands and knees, and soap powder all over her head, went round to the front gate to see if anyone else might be doing anything interesting.

A cat was sitting washing itself on the wall outside. Mary-Mary opened the gate, stroked the cat, and looked around.

The coal cart was standing a few doors away, outside Mr

"You're spilling it!"

Bassett's house. The coalman wasn't there, but Mr Bassett was walking round and round the cart talking to himself. Every now and then he stooped down and tried to look underneath it, but he was a big, fat man, and it was difficult for him to bend easily in the middle.

Mary-Mary wondered what he was doing, and who he was talking to. The coalman's horse was eating out of a nosebag and didn't seem to be taking any notice of him.

Mary-Mary moved a little nearer.

Mr Bassett straightened his back, looked at the horse with a worried face, and said, "Puss, puss."

"It isn't a cat. It's a horse," said Mary-Mary.

Mr Bassett turned and saw her.

"Ah, Mary-Mary!" he said. "You're a much better size

than I am. Do you mind looking under the coal cart and telling me what you can see there?"

Mary-Mary bent down.

"I can see a lump of coal," she said.

"Anything else?" said Mr Bassett.

"Yes," said Mary-Mary, "quite a lot of things. There's another lump of coal and a silver pencil and a piece of paper—"

"Isn't there a cat there?" asked Mr Bassett.

"No," said Mary-Mary.

"Are you sure?" said Mr Bassett.

"Yes, quite sure," said Mary-Mary, "but there's a cat sitting on the wall over there if you really want one."

Mr Bassett looked up and saw the cat washing itself on the wall.

"Well I never!" he said. "It must have run out when I wasn't looking. I saw it go under the cart as I came out of the gate, and I was afraid it might get run over when the coalman came back. I bent down to call it out, but it wouldn't come. Then I felt something fall out of my pocket, but I was more worried about the cat."

Mary-Mary liked Mr Bassett. It was kind of him to be so worried about the cat.

"Shall I fetch out what you dropped?" she asked. "I can get under the cart more easily than you can."

"Won't you get dirty?"

Mary-Mary looked down at herself

"I don't think I could get much dirtier than I am," she said.

"No, perhaps not," said Mr Bassett. "It's very kind of you."

So Mary-Mary crawled underneath the back of the coal cart, and Mr Bassett stood by waiting.

"Oh!" called Mary-Mary, "there's half a crown down here as well!"

"Good," said Mr Bassett. "Bring out everything you see. I can't be quite sure what fell out of my pocket."

So Mary-Mary picked up the half-crown and the two lumps of coal and the piece of paper and the silver pencil, and crawled out again.

"Good girl," said Mr Bassett. "Now let's sort them out. These two lumps of coal belong to the coalman, so we'll throw them back on the cart, and the silver pencil belongs to me, so I'll put it in my pocket. The paper doesn't belong to anybody, so we'll throw it away, and the half-crown—well—I think the half-crown belongs to you, because you've earned it."

"How did I earn it?" said Mary-Mary.

"By being just the right size to fetch it out," said Mr Bassett. "What would you like to spend it on?"

Mary-Mary said, "I've been thinking all the morning that if I had threepence I'd spend it on an ice lolly."

Mr Bassett began counting on his fingers.

"We could buy ten ice lollies with this half-crown," he said, "but I think that's too many, don't you? Let's go and spend it, anyway. Shall we go to that nice little teashop on the corner?"

"Oh, yes," said Mary-Mary. "I'd like to go there very much. That's where I go to watch the ladies sitting in the window drinking their coffee. It's next to the ice-lolly shop.

I've always wanted to look like one of those ladies."

"Very well," said Mr Bassett, "so you shall."

Mary-Mary looked down at herself.

"I'm rather dirty to look like a lady," she said.

"And I'm rather fat, and don't look like a lady, either," said Mr Bassett. "But if we feel right and behave right I don't suppose anyone will notice what we look like. You don't shout and throw things about, do you?"

"Not usually," said Mary-Mary.

"Or lick your plate?"

"Not when I'm out," said Mary-Mary.

"Nor do I," said Mr Bassett, "so we ought to be all right."

So Mary-Mary, with her skirt still rather damp, decorated with dust and tea-leaves, with shoe-polish on her hands and knees, soap powder all over her hair, and a smudge of coal-dust on the end of her nose, went walking politely down the road with Mr Bassett to the nice little teashop.

"We will order one very large ice-cream sundae, and one cup of tea," said Mr Bassett.

"Which will be for which?" asked Mary-Mary politely.

"I shall order the ice-cream sundae for myself," said Mr Bassett, "because I like ice-cream sundaes very much. But I am not allowed to eat them, because they make me too fat, so you shall eat it for me and I shall watch you."

"I don't like tea very much," said Mary-Mary.

"Then I shall drink it for you," said Mr Bassett, "and we shall suit each other very nicely."

When Miriam and Martyn and Mervyn and Meg had finished the dustbins, polishing the shoes, and washing the

They all looked into the window—

clothes they were all very hot and tired.

"What shall we spend our threepences on?" said Miriam.

"Something cool," said Martyn.

"Ice lollies," said Mervyn.

"Good idea," said Meg.

"But you'd better tidy yourselves up before you go out," said Mother.

So Miriam and Martyn and Mervyn and Meg washed their hands and brushed their hair, and then they all set off together to buy their ice lollies.

Miriam chose a raspberry flavour, Martyn chose a strawberry, Mervyn chose an orange one, and Meg chose a lime.

Then they all stood in a row, sucking them, and looked

into the window of the nice little teashop. And suddenly they all opened their eyes very wide and said, "Look!" all together, for there at the table in the window sat Mary-Mary, looking quite at home, just as if she were a lady drinking her morning coffee; only Mary-Mary wasn't drinking coffee—she was eating a very large ice-cream sundae out of a very tall glass, with a very long spoon.

"It's Mary-Mary!" they all said together.

"With shoe-polish on her hands!"

"And soap powder in her hair!"

"And coal-dust on her nose!"

"And a whacking great ice-cream sundae! Now, however did she get that?"

Mary-Mary waved to them all with the long spoon and felt very pleased to be sitting on the right side of the window for a change. But Miriam and Martyn and Mervyn and Meg didn't seem to want to wave back to her, so she started talking to Mr Bassett again.

"It's much nicer being on the inside looking out," she said.

"Nicer than what?" said Mr Bassett.

"Being on the outside looking in," said Mary-Mary.

"Oh, yes," said Mr Bassett, "much nicer."

He was sitting with his back to the window, so he hadn't seen the others looking in.

"You know, I'm beginning to feel rather sorry for all my brothers and sisters," Mary-Mary went on.

"Why is that?" said Mr Bassett.

"Well," said Mary-Mary, "they earned threepence each today (that's enough to buy an ice lolly), and they kept

—there sat Mary-Mary

telling me I could earn threepence too when I was as big as they are. But if *they'd* been only as big as *me* they might have earned half a crown and been sitting in here with us, mightn't they?"

"Yes, I suppose they might," said Mr Bassett, "but, of course, there's no need to tell them, unless you want to."

"Oh, no, I won't tell them," said Mary-Mary, smiling to herself.

So Mary-Mary did earn some money after all, and that is the end of the story.

3

Mary-Mary's Handbag

ONE day Mary-Mary found a lady's handbag in the dustbin. It was large and flat and shabby, but it opened and shut nicely with a loud snap, and there was a pocket inside which was just the right size for Moppet.

"I'll keep this," said Mary-Mary. "It will come in very handy, and I'm sure the dustman won't need it."

So she took it away and played with it, and opened it and shut it, and put things in it and took them out again, and was very pleased with her find.

"Whatever have you got there?" said Miriam.

"More old rubbish, I expect," said Martyn.

"Why, it's Mother's old handbag!" said Mervyn.

"The one before last," said Meg.

Then they all said together, "Throw it away, Mary-Mary. It's only old rubbish."

But Mary-Mary said, "Different things suit different people. A grown-up lady's handbag suits me very well,"

- very pleased with her find

and she would not throw it away.

A little later Miriam was out with her friend, Barbara, when she saw Mary-Mary walking down the road with the handbag on her arm.

Oh, dear! thought Miriam. How awful she looks!

"Mary-Mary," she said, "if you'll only throw that dreadful old handbag away I'll give you something else."

"What will you give me?" said Mary-Mary.

Miriam said, "I'll give you the little basket that my Easter egg was in. It's much prettier than that old thing."

"All right. When will you give it me?" said Mary-Mary.

"When I come home," said Miriam. "I'm just going out with Barbara now, but I'll give it you when I get back. Now go home like a good girl and put that dreadful bag in the dustbin."

So Mary-Mary went on up the road towards home.

Mary-Mary had to run to keep up

Martyn and Mervyn were just coming out of the gate.

"Where are you going?" said Mary-Mary.

"To the sweetshop, to spend our pocket money," they said.

"I'll come with you," said Mary-Mary.

"No, not with that awful old handbag," said Martyn.

"Everyone will laugh at you," said Mervyn.

"*I* don't mind," said Mary-Mary, walking after them.

"No, but we do," said Martyn and Mervyn, and they walked even quicker, so that Mary-Mary had to run to keep up.

"Can't you see we want to be by ourselves?" said Martyn.

"All right, I won't interrupt you," said Mary-Mary.

"Let's pretend we don't know her," said Mervyn, and they ran on ahead.

When Mary-Mary got to the sweetshop Martyn and Mervyn were standing by the counter waiting to be served.

Mary-Mary went in and stood beside them. They pretended not to notice her.

A lady in front of them was taking a long time buying a box of chocolates. After a while Mary-Mary got tired of waiting and began opening and shutting her handbag with such loud snaps that every one looked round to see what the noise was. Martyn and Mervyn pretended not to hear.

At last the lady chose her box of chocolates, and the shopman said, "That will be ten and sixpence, please."

The lady opened her handbag and looked inside.

"I'm afraid I haven't any change," she said, and gave the shopman a pound note.

When she had gone the shop man turned to Martyn.

"Are you all together?" he asked.

"No," said Mary-Mary, "these boys are by themselves."

"Then I'll serve you first as you're the smallest," said the shopman. "What would you like?"

"I'd like two halfpenny chews," said Mary-Mary.

She opened the dreadful handbag and looked inside. "But I'm afraid I haven't any change," she said.

"Now, look here, Mary-Mary," said Martyn, "if we buy you two halfpenny chews will you go home and put that awful old thing in the dustbin?"

"What awful old thing?" said Mary-Mary in a loud, surprised voice. "Do you mean my handbag?"

"Yes," said Martyn, "but don't talk so loud."

"All right," said Mary-Mary, "of course I will, if you'll buy me two halfpenny chews."

"You go on home, then," said Martyn.

So Mary-Mary went on up the road towards home again. Meg was just coming out of the door as she got there.

"Where are you going?" said Mary-Mary.

"To see my music teacher about the concert on Friday," said Meg.

"Perhaps I'll come with you," said Mary-Mary.

"Not with that dreadful old bag," said Meg. "Why don't you throw it away? If you'll put it in the dustbin I'll give you my little red purse."

"Oh, thank you," said Mary-Mary. And she went indoors, wrapped her dreadful old handbag carefully in newspaper, and put it in the dustbin.

Martyn and Mervyn came home first.

"Where is that old handbag?" they said.

"In the dustbin," said Mary-Mary.

"Good," they said, and gave her two halfpenny chews. Miriam came home next.

"Did you do as I said?" she asked.

"Yes," said Mary-Mary.

"Good girl," said Miriam, and gave her the little basket. Meg came home last.

"Well, is it in the dustbin?" she asked.

"Yes," said Mary-Mary, "it's been there a long time."

"Good," said Meg, and gave her the little red purse.

Early next morning Mary-Mary saw the dustman coming up the road with his lorry.

Oh, dear! she thought, it would be a pity if he should throw my handbag in among all the ashes and rubbish. It would spoil it.

Mary-Mary ran out to the dustbin, dug the handbag out from under some potato peelings, and buried it in the sand-pit. Then, when the dustman had gone, she wrapped it up again in fresh newspaper and put it carefully back in the dustbin.

On the day of the music teacher's concert Miriam, Martyn, Mervyn, and Meg were all waiting to go, when Mother said, "Where is Mary-Mary? I got her ready first on purpose so that we shouldn't be late. Where can she be?"

"I saw her digging in the sand-pit just now," said Father, "but don't you wait. I'll bring her along with me."

So Miriam, Martyn, Mervyn, and Meg all went off with Mother, and Father followed later with Mary-Mary.

The concert was just going to begin when suddenly there was a loud snap from the back of the hall. Everyone looked round, and there was Mary-Mary, smiling brightly, with the dreadful-looking handbag on her arm.

"*Well!*" said Miriam, Martyn, Mervyn, and Meg, all together.

As soon as the concert was over they all ran up to her.

"Didn't I give you a little basket?" said Miriam.

"Didn't we give you two halfpenny chews?" said Martyn and Mervyn.

"Didn't I give you my little red purse?" said Meg.

"Yes. Thank you," said Mary-Mary, "and I've got them all in here. This is such a handy handbag, it's big enough to hold everything. I've even got Moppet in the pocket. He did enjoy the concert."

"But you said you'd put it in the dustbin!" they said, all

together.

"Yes, and I did," said Mary-Mary, "but it was a silly place to keep a handbag. I had to keep washing my hands every time I dug it out, so I don't keep it there any more."

So Mary-Mary kept her dreadful handbag after all, and that is the end of the story.

4

Mary-Mary Goes Away

ONE day Mary-Mary's mother had to go out for the whole afternoon, so Mary-Mary stayed at home with all her big brothers and sisters.

"What are we going to do?" said Mary-Mary. "Shall we do something nice?"

But Miriam said, "I know what I'm going to do. I've got to write a letter."

And Martyn said, "I know what I'm going to do, too. I'm going to paint a picture."

Mervyn said, "I'm going to make a cut-out model." And Meg said, "I've got to do my sums. I didn't finish them yesterday, so I've got to do them today. It isn't fair, but I suppose I'd better do them, all the same."

Miriam went into the bedroom to write her letter (because she couldn't think with everyone talking to her), and Martyn went into the kitchen (because it was handier for changing the paint water), and Mervyn went into the dining-room (because he needed the table to lay his model out on), and Meg went into the sitting-room (because she said she might as well sit in a comfortable chair, even if she did have to do sums on a Saturday).

Mary-Mary followed them from room to room, but they all said, "Oh, do go away, Mary-Mary." "You're interrupting." "Don't be a nuisance." "Leave us alone."

So Mary-Mary went next door to see Miss Summers. But Miss Summers was busy too. She said, "I'm so sorry, Mary-Mary, but I've no time for visitors today, because I'm going away."

"Where are you going?" asked Mary-Mary.

"To stay with a friend," said Miss Summers.

"How long for?" asked Mary-Mary.

"I haven't quite decided yet," said Miss Summers. "I'll see how I like it. Just now I'm busy getting ready."

Mary-Mary went home again, and went up to the bedroom.

"Miriam," she said, "I won't talk to you while you're writing your letter, but will you tell me when you've finished writing it so that I can talk to you? Because I shan't know how long to go on not interrupting you if you don't tell me when you've finished, and it would be a pity to go on not talking if you had finished, wouldn't it?"

Miriam said, "Oh, do stop talking, Mary-Mary, and go away!"

So Mary-Mary went down into the kitchen and said, "Martyn, will you tell me when you've finished painting so that I shall know when I won't be interrupting you?"

But Martyn said, "Oh, go away, Mary-Mary!"

Then Mary-Mary went into the dining-room.

"Mervyn," she said, "I know you haven't finished making your model yet, so I won't interrupt you; but will you tell me when you have finished, because then I shall be able to come and see it without interrupting you, and if I don't know when you've finishd I might come and interrupt you without meaning to?

"You're interrupting me now," said Mervyn. "Go away!"

So Mary-Mary went into the sitting-room to see Meg, but before she had time to say a word Meg looked up crossly and said, "Go *away*, Mary-Mary!" So Mary-Mary went.

"That's funny," she said to herself. "They all said the same thing. Every one of them told me to go away."

She stood in the hall for a minute, thinking hard, then she went next door again.

Miss Summers, in her best hat, was just coming out of the house.

Mary-Mary said, "Do you mind telling me before you go what you had to do to get ready to go away?"

"Oh, all sorts of things," said Miss Summers. "Pack my bag, leave a note for the milkman, lock the back door—why do you want to know?"

"I might be going away myself," said Mary-Mary, "and it's useful to know."

"But you can't go away by yourself until you're grown up," said Miss Summers.

"Why not?" said Mary-Mary.

"Because little girls can't," said Miss Summers. "You'll

have to wait till you're a grown-up lady."

She kissed Mary-Mary good-bye.

"I'll probably be back on Tuesday," she said, "then you must come and see me again."

Mary-Mary went home again, thinking hard all the way.

Miriam was half-way through her letter when the door opened, and Mary-Mary looked in with a tea-cosy on her head.

"Does this look like a lady's hat?" she asked.

Miriam laughed. "It does rather," she said.

"Do I look like a grown-up lady?"

"No," said Miriam, "you haven't got ladies' shoes on."

Mary-Mary went away and tried on several pairs of Mother's shoes. They were all rather large.

But I'll soon get used to that, she said to herself.

She chose a pair with high heels, because they made her look taller, and carried them downstairs in her hand. Then she put them on and hobbled into the kitchen where Martyn was still busy painting.

"Do I look like a grown-up lady?" she asked.

Martyn laughed. "You might if your skirt was longer," he said.

Mary-Mary slipped the straps of her skirt over her shoulders so that her skirt fell down nearly to her ankles. Then she hobbled away to find Mervyn, who was still busy with his model.

"Do I look like a lady who's going away?" said Mary-Mary.

Mervyn looked up.

"Jolly nearly," he said, laughing. "But where's your

handbag?"

"Oh, yes—my handbag! I quite forgot!" said Mary-Mary, and she went away and dug it up out of the sand-pit.

Then, with the tea-cosy on her head, Mother's shoes on her feet, her skirt almost down to her ankles, and her dreadful-looking handbag over her arm, she went off to find Meg.

Meg was still busy with her sums. She was frowning, thinking hard, and counting on her fingers.

"Do I look like a grown-up lady?" asked Mary-Mary.

Meg went on frowning and counting, not looking up.

Mary-Mary asked her again.

"Oh, *go away*!" said Meg.

"Yes. Good-bye," said Mary-Mary.

Meg looked up, surprised, but Mary-Mary had gone.

She had gone to the cupboard under the stairs to get a paper carrier bag. After that she fetched her toothbrush and a nightie and Moppet. She wrapped them up in a small bundle of comics and put them in the carrier bag.

Then she wrote a note for the milkman. It said, "Dear Milkman, I've gone away, love from Mary-Mary." After that she locked the back door. Then she was ready.

She stopped in the hall to say good-bye to herself in the mirror.

"I shall probably be back on Tuesday," she said.

"Very well, madam," she answered herself. "Have a nice time."

"Thank you," said Mary-Mary, and stepped out into the street.

– and stepped out into the street

A boy was sitting on the wall on the other side of the road.
When he saw Mary-Mary come out of the house wearing
her tea-cosy hat, her high-heeled shoes, and with her skirt
nearly down to her ankles he stared hard. Then he whistled.
Then he laughed out loud.

Mary-Mary took no notice of him and started walking
carefully down the road. But her shoes slipped this way
and that, and it was difficult not to turn her ankle over, so
after a while she stepped out of them and put them in the
carrier bag.

The boy got off the wall and followed her down on the
other side of the road.

"Where do you think you're going?" he called.

"I'm going away," said Mary-Mary.

"I don't believe it," said the boy. "Where to?"

"To stay with a friend," said Mary-Mary.

"Yah!" said the boy. "I don't believe it."

And he sat down on the wall to watch which way she would go.

Mary-Mary had been in such a hurry to get out without anyone seeing her that she had forgotten to make up her mind where she was going. She began thinking quickly which of her friends she could be going to stay with. Miss Summers had gone away, so it was no good going there. Mrs Merry had no spare bed. Mary-Mary decided that Mr Bassett would be very glad to have her. She turned in at his gate, put on her shoes, and rang the front-door bell.

"I bet you didn't really ring the bell!" shouted the boy.

Mr Bassett's front door opened. Mary-Mary turned round quickly, made a face at the boy, and stepped inside with a polite cough. Mr Bassett himself had opened the door.

"Dear me!" he said, looking down at her. "Where are you going? You look as if you're going away."

"Yes, I am. I'm going to stay with you," said Mary-Mary.

"Are you really? How long for?"

"I haven't quite decided yet. We'll see how I like it, shall we?" said Mary-Mary.

"Dear, dear!" said Mr Bassett. "Well, you'd better come in."

He took her into the front room, and Mary-Mary sat on the edge of a large leather armchair.

"Would you like to take your hat off?" asked Mr Bassett.

Mary-Mary took it off, and Mr Bassett put it on the

"I've come to stay with you"

sideboard.

"It looks rather like a tea-cosy on there, doesn't it?" said Mary-Mary.

"Yes," said Mr Bassett, "I almost thought it was one. Perhaps we'd better hang it on a peg."

"No, it's all right," said Mary-Mary, "don't bother. It can go in this bag with my toothbrush and nightie."

"Toothbrush and nightie?" said Mr Bassett. "Do you mean you're going to sleep here?"

"Yes," said Mary-Mary.

"But I didn't ask you, did I?"

Mary-Mary thought hard.

"Do people have to be asked before they go away?" she said.

"They do usually."

"Oh, dear!" said Mary-Mary. "And I forgot to ask you to ask me. You'd better ask me now, hadn't you?"

Mr Bassett sat down and wrote her an invitation which said, "Dear Mary-Mary, Please will you come and stay with me from two to four o'clock today. I shall be so pleased if you will."

"Thank you," said Mary-Mary. "I shall like to come very much. But why only till four?"

"I don't like planning things too far ahead," said Mr Bassett.

"How funny," said Mary-Mary. "I like looking forward to things. Never mind—you can write me another invitation at four o'clock asking me to stay till Tuesday. What shall we do now?"

"We could play ludo," said Mr Bassett. "Or would you like to come and see my rabbits?"

"Oh, do you keep rabbits?" said Mary-Mary. "I *am* glad."

"Yes," said Mr Bassett, "and the people next door keep chickens. But I like rabbits better."

"You're lucky," said Mary-Mary. "My father and mother only keep children. I like rabbits better too. Let's go and see them first, and we can play ludo after. That will be very nice."

So Mary-Mary went into the garden with Mr Bassett and fed the rabbits and played with them, and after that they settled down to ludo.

By this time Miriam and Martyn and Mervyn and Meg had finished writing and painting and cutting out and counting. They looked around for Mary-Mary, but she was nowhere to be seen. They looked upstairs and downstairs and all round the garden, but they couldn't find her anywhere. Then Miriam went out of the back door and found the note to the milkman inside the empty milk bottle. She read it, then she shouted to the others, and they all came running.

"She's gone away!" said Miriam.

"Where to?" said Martyn.

"Doesn't she say?" said Mervyn.

"How silly!" said Meg.

Then they all said together, "Oh, dear! Whatever will Mother say?" And they began to get really worried.

They went down the road, looking in at the windows of all the shops and asking everyone they knew. A boy was standing outside the sweetshop sucking a liquorice pipe.

"Have you seen a little girl come this way?" they asked him. "With a bag?" "And a hat?" "And a pair of shoes?"

"Yes," said the boy, "and jolly funny she looked. Said she was going away to stay with a friend. She went into the old gent's house up there."

Very relieved, they all went up the road again to Mr Bassett's house, the boy following them. He sat on the wall to watch what would happen, and Miriam, Martyn, Mervyn, and Meg rang the bell.

Mary-Mary opened the door. She looked very surprised to see them.

"You naughty girl!" they all said together. "We've been

"Please will you come back?"

looking for you everywhere."

"Come home at once."

"You shouldn't have gone away."

Mary-Mary shut the door. Then she said through the letter-box, "You shouldn't shout outside other people's houses. I'm ashamed of you."

"Mary-Mary, you must come home!" called Miriam.

"No," said Mary-Mary, "you told me to go away, and I've gone away."

"Open the door," said Miriam.

"No," said Mary-Mary.

"Where is Mr Bassett?" said Martyn.

"He's playing ludo and mustn't be disturbed," said Mary-Mary.

"Let us in," said Mervyn.

"No, said Mary-Mary.

43

"Mother will be coming home soon," said Meg. "You *must* come back. We're supposed to be looking after you."

"I'm not coming back," said Mary-Mary.

The others all whispered together in a worried sort of way, and the boy on the wall laughed rudely.

Then Miriam said, "Mary-Mary, dear, I'm sorry we all told you to go away. Will you come back now?"

There was silence for a moment, then Mary-Mary opened the door.

"*Please* will you come back?" they said, all together.

Mary-Mary smiled.

"I don't think I'll come back," she said, "but I might come and stay with you if you ask me properly."

"All right—please will you come and stay with us?"

"Will you treat me like a visitor?"

"We'll try," they said.

"What will there be for tea?"

Miriam thought quickly and said, "Sardine sandwiches." (They were Mary-Mary's favourite.)

"Will you remember to say, 'Take two as they're so small'?"

"Don't be silly," said Miriam.

Mary-Mary started to shut the door again.

"I'm sorry I can't come and stay with you today," she said. "Perhaps some other time—"

But Martyn held the door open, and Miriam said, "Yes, yes—take two as they're so small. Take three if you like. But do please come home—I mean, do please come and stay with us!"

– the boy on the wall laughed rudely

"Very well," said Mary-Mary; "as you all want me so much, I'll come. But I must just go and pack my things. You can go on if you like and start getting tea ready for me."

So Miriam, Martyn, Mervyn, and Meg went home (the boy on the wall laughed rudely as they went by), and Mary-Mary went and told Mr Bassett she was sorry she couldn't stay any longer, but her family very much wanted her to go and stay with them for a while.

She put on her shoes and her tea-cosy hat, and Mr Bassett saw her to the door.

On the doorstep she stopped to make sure she had got everything. She brought out the small bundle of comics.

"You might like to keep these," she said. "I brought them to read in bed, but I've got plenty more at home."

"Thank you very much," said Mr Bassett.

"And thank you for having me," said Mary-Mary.

Miriam, Martyn, Mervyn, and Meg all came out to their own doorstep.

"Tea is nearly ready," they called. "We shall be so pleased if you will come."

"Thank you, I will," said Mary-Mary, and she set off down the steps.

The rude boy was still sitting on the wall.

"That was one up to you, wasn't it?" he said, laughing.

"I don't know what you mean," said Mary-Mary.

"Go on!" said the boy. "Of course you do. Everybody knows what 'one up to you' means!"

"I'm sure *I* don't," said Mary-Mary, and hobbled carefully up to her own front door, where all her big brothers and sisters were politely waiting for her.

So Mary-Mary went away and then came home again to stay, and that is the end of the story.

5

Mary-Mary is a Surprise

ONE day Mary-Mary sat at the table giving Moppet his breakfast. She sat him beside her plate with one cornflake in front of his nose, and while she was waiting for him to eat it she listened to all her big brothers and sisters talking.

"Mrs Merry's party is going to be lovely," said Miriam. "It isn't going to end until half-past midnight."

"Smashing," said Martyn.

"Super," said Mervyn.

"Golly!" said Meg.

"We've never been to such a late party before," said Miriam. "I suppose it's because it's a New Year party."

"Whizzo," said Martyn.

"Hooray," said Mervyn.

"Gorgeous!" said Meg.

Mary-Mary was very surprised to hear that there was going to be a party.

"When are we going?" she asked.

But all the others said, "No, not you, Mary-Mary." "It's only us." "You weren't asked." "You're too little."

Mary-Mary moved Moppet's nose a little closer to his cornflake and didn't say anything.

"Never mind," said Miriam.

"Wait till you're bigger," said Martyn.

"Then you'll be able to go too," said Mervyn.

"If anyone asks you," said Meg.

And they all said, "Never mind, Mary-Mary," together.

Mary-Mary got down from her place and said in a busy and rather worried voice, "I couldn't have gone, anyway. I am far too busy. Moppet has a cold and he needs looking after."

She gave a tiny sneeze in Moppet's voice and looked at the cornflake.

"You see, he hasn't even eaten his breakfast. I have to eat it for him."

She put the cornflake in her mouth, then, still looking busy and worried, she carried Moppet away and put him to bed in a small cardboard box.

All the morning, while the others talked about the New Year party and what they should wear and who would fetch them home and what there would be to eat, Moppet's cold got worse and worse.

Mary-Mary sat with him and told him stories and tucked him up in cotton-wool and gave him medicine from a doll's tea-cup, and was so busy that she had no time at all to think about the party.

"Once upon a time there were two huge great fairies."

About an hour before dinner-time Mrs Merry came in on her way back from shopping. She was a fat, jolly lady whom they all liked; but as soon as Mary-Mary heard her voice in the hall she hid under the table with Moppet. She didn't want to see Mrs Merry today.

Miriam, Martyn, Mervyn, and Meg brought Mrs Merry into the dining-room, and they all started talking about the New Year party all over again.

"I have a lovely plan," said Mrs Merry. "I am going to dress Mr Merry up as a very old man, with a long white beard—to be the Old Year, you know. Then, when the clock strikes midnight (and it really is the end of the year), I thought how lovely it would be if we could have two or three fairies come in with a great big box of crackers to give away to everybody to wish them a Happy New Year."

"Fairies?" said Meg.

"Not real fairies," said Mrs Merry, "and that's what I've come about. I wanted to ask you if you'd like to help. We shall need quite big people, because I'm planning to have a really huge box of crackers. Now, how would you like to be the fairies?"

"Oh, yes!" said Miriam.

"What—me?" said Martyn.

"Oh, no!" said Mervyn.

"Oh, *yes*!" said Meg.

"No, not you boys," said Mrs Merry. "I meant Miriam and Meg."

Martyn and Mervyn looked relieved, and Miriam and Meg were delighted.

"But what shall we wear?" they said.

Mrs Merry said she had two fairy dresses that would just fit them.

"They used to belong to Barbara and Bunty," she said, "but the dresses are too small now, and, anyway, Barbara and Bunty have grown too fat to be fairies any more—so we thought it would be lovely if you two would do it. But don't tell anyone. It is to be a surprise."

Mary-Mary, under the table, said to Moppet, "Shall I tell you a story? Once upon a time there were two huge great fairies—"

"Mary-Mary!" said Miriam. "Go away at once. You shouldn't have been listening."

"—and their names both began with an M—" went on Mary-Mary.

"Oh, do go away!" said Miriam and Meg.

"—they were called Margarine and Marmalade—" said Mary-Mary.

"Shall we push her out?" said Martyn.

"Take me away!" said Mary-Mary in Moppet's voice. "I don't believe in fairies—I only believe in mice."

Mary-Mary crawled out from under the table, saying to Moppet, "Very well, I'll take you away and tell you a mouse story." And she went into the kitchen where Mother was busy cooking the dinner.

Mary-Mary sat under the draining-board and told Moppet his mouse story, which went like this, "Once upon a time there was a poor little mouse who had a very bad cold, and it got worse and worse, until somebody gave him an ice-cream, and then all of a sudden it got better."

Mother looked up from her cooking.

"How bad is Moppet's cold now?" she asked.

"It is a bit worse," said Mary-Mary, "but I don't think he'll die of it—at least, not yet—at least, I *hope* not."

"Do you think an ice-cream would help him?" asked Mother.

"Oh, yes," said Mary-Mary. "What a good idea!"

So Mother gave her threepence, and Mary-Mary ran down to the shop and bought an ice-cream. On the way back she saw Mrs Merry coming down the road.

"I mustn't stop and talk to her," said Mary-Mary to herself. "I must hurry home to my poor child, Moppet, who has such a nasty cold. I will talk to her another day."

So she put her head down and began to run. She was

hoping that if she ran fast enough Mrs Merry wouldn't have time to see who it was. But Mrs Merry called out, "Why, Mary-Mary! You're just the person I want to see." So Mary-Mary had to stop, after all.

"You heard all about the plan for my party, didn't you?" said Mrs Merry. "Well, I'm planning a surprise at the end that I didn't tell the others about. I need someone very little to help me do it, and you're just the person I want. Now, will you come to my party secretly, without anyone knowing? Mr Merry will fetch you in the car while the party is going on. I have a lovely little dress for you to wear, and I want you to come as the big surprise when the clock strikes midnight. Do you think you would like to be the surprise at my party?"

"Oh, yes!" said Mary-Mary. "I've quite often been a surprise by mistake, but it would be very nice to be a surprise on purpose."

"I've asked your mother," said Mrs Merry, "and she says it will be quite all right. She knows all about it and she's not going to tell any of the others; so you mustn't either. Come to tea with me today, and we will plan it together."

Mary-Mary ran home feeling very pleased indeed. Moppet's ice-cream was nearly melted by the time she got there, so she gave it to him in a tea-cup. She sang so loudly while she was helping him to eat it that Miriam, Martyn, Mervyn, and Meg were quite surprised.

"Why is Mary-Mary so happy all of a sudden?" they said.

"Mrs Merry has asked her to tea today," said Mother.

"Oh, because she can't go to the party!" they said.

"I must hurry home to my poor child, Moppet."

"Is Moppet's cold better now?" asked Mother.

"Quite, quite better," said Mary-Mary, licking up the last of the ice-cream. "I knew it would be."

When New Year's Eve came Miriam, Martyn, Mervyn, and Meg were all very excited. Mary-Mary watched them getting ready for the party and tried not to look excited too.

She went to bed in her underclothes, with a nightie on top so that the others wouldn't guess. (She was going to have supper on a tray when they had gone, and Mother had promised to read her a story until it was time for Mr Merry to come and fetch her.)

When they were ready to go Miriam, Martyn, Mervyn, and Meg all came to say good-night to her. Mary-Mary hid under the blankets, because she couldn't help laughing, and they thought she was hiding because she was sad about not going to the party. So they were all very kind to her.

"Never mind, Mary-Mary," they said. "When you're

bigger you will be able to go to a New Year party too."

Miriam said, "Don't cry. I'll give you one of my party hair ribbons tomorrow."

Martyn said, "Cheer up, and I'll bring you back something nice to eat."

Mervyn said, "I'll save you my paper serviette. It will make a tablecloth for Moppet."

And Meg said, "Go to sleep now, like a good girl, and I'll tell you all about it in the morning."

Mary-Mary (still under the blankets) said, "Thank you" and "Good-bye" and "Have a nice time"; and then off they all went.

It was a lovely party. Miriam, Martyn, Mervyn, and Meg had a very jolly time.

A little while before midnight Miriam and Meg slipped away to put on their fairy clothes. As they ran through the hall on their way upstairs they saw Mr Merry just coming in at the front door with a great big round box in his arms.

"Hallo!" he said. "Are you having a good time?"

"Oh, yes!" they said, both together.

"And where are the rest of your family?" asked Mr Merry.

"Martyn and Mervyn are in the sitting-room with the others," said Miriam.

"And Mary-Mary is fast asleep in bed," said Meg.

"Why?" said Mr Merry. "Has she been naughty?"

"Oh, no!" said Miriam and Meg together, "but she's *much* too little to come to a New Year party."

"You two are going to be the fairies, aren't you?" said Mr Merry.

– carrying a large round box between them

"Yes," they said. "Are those the crackers in that box? Can we see?"

"Not to be opened till midnight!" said Mr Merry, laughing. "You will be careful not to drop it, won't you? It is heavier than you might think."

He carried the box into the kitchen and shut the door, and Miriam and Meg ran on upstairs to change.

In the sitting-room Martyn and Mervyn were very busy. Mrs Merry had put them in charge of the games (with Billy and Bob to help them) while she went away to see to one or two things. Barbara and Bunty were seeing to the refreshments.

They had just finished a game of Blind Man's Buff when Mrs Merry came back, looking very jolly.

"What time is it?" she asked.

"It's nearly midnight!" shouted all the children, pointing at the clock.

"So it is!" said Mrs Merry. "Now, stand back, all of you, and make a way through. I believe I hear someone coming."

Everyone stood back. Then the door opened and in came a very old man with a long white beard. He limped across the room, leaning heavily on a stick, and peered up at the clock.

"Who is he?" somebody whispered.

Everyone started talking at once. "I know! He's the Old Year!" "How wonderful!" "And he's looking at the clock, because he's only got another minute left!" (But hardly anyone guessed it was really Mr Merry dressed up.)

As the clock began striking twelve the old man turned and hobbled out of the room. At the same minute there was the sound of bells ringing, and two fairies came running in, carrying a large round box between them. They looked so pretty in their pink-and-blue dresses with silver wings that every one started clapping and saying, "Oh, aren't they lovely!" (But hardly anyone guessed it was really Miriam and Meg.)

The fairies put the big box down on the floor and smiled and curtseyed. Then, on the last stroke of twelve, they bent down and lifted the lid.

"OH!" cried everyone, "Oh, just look! How *sweet*!" For there, rising out of the box with her arms full of crackers, was the sweetest little fairy person. She was wearing a short white frock and a silver crown with a star on her head.

"It's the little New Year!" they all cried. "Oh, *isn't* she

sweet? What a lovely idea! Who can she be?"

And, of course, it was Mary-Mary!

"Happy New Year, everybody!" she called, and, climbing out of the box, she threw the crackers to everyone.

Miriam and Meg, as well as Martyn and Mervyn, could hardly believe their eyes.

"It's Mary-Mary!" they all said. "However did she get here?" "We left her at home in bed!" "But doesn't she look pretty!"

And after a while, when they had stopped being quite so

surprised, they began to feel rather proud of Mary-Mary.

Everyone began asking who the sweet little girl really was, and Miriam, Martyn, Mervyn, and Meg wandered around saying, "Oh, that's our little sister, Mary-Mary."

"Didn't you know she was coming?" someone asked.

"No," they said. "We *were* surprised. Yes, she is rather sweet, isn't she? We're quite proud of her."

Mary-Mary, sitting on Mrs Merry's lap, eating a chocolate ice-cream, heard all this and smiled to herself. She was rather surprised too.

So Mary-Mary did go to the New Year party after all,
and that is the end of the story.

More
Mary-
Mary

For SYLVIA MAY

Contents

1

Mary-Mary Has a Photograph Taken

MARY-MARY was the youngest of five. All her brothers and sisters were very big and clever, and knew all about everything; but Mary-Mary didn't know much about anything. So all her big brothers and sisters, who were called Miriam, Martyn, Mervyn, and Meg, used to tell her what to do and how to do it. But Mary-Mary liked doing things her own way. So she used to say, "No, I shan't. I'll do it the other way."

And that, of course, is why she was called Mary-Mary instead of just Mary, which was her real name.

One day Mary-Mary's mother said, "I think it is time you had your photographs taken again. We haven't had a proper one done since you were all quite little."

"Mary-Mary is still quite little," said Miriam.

"But she was a baby last time," said Martyn.

"And she kept wriggling and screeching," said Mervyn.

"And pulling my hair-ribbon," said Meg.

Then they all started talking at once, saying, "Don't let's have our photographs taken all together." "Let's each have one of our own." "Then they can all go in separate frames."

But Mother said, "I'm afraid that would cost far too much. Besides, I should like to have one of all five of you. Then I could put it on top of my writing-desk, where all my friends could see it."

"What shall we wear?" said Miriam.

"Jeans and a jersey," said Martyn.

"Space suits," said Mervyn.

"My party dress," said Meg.

"I shan't wear anything," said Mary-Mary.

"*What!*" said all the others.

"Anything special, I mean," said Mary-Mary.

Mother said she didn't think it mattered much what they wore so long as they were all clean and tidy, and remembered to smile and look pleasant.

"You will have to sit quite still, Mary-Mary," said Miriam.

"And not make silly faces," said Martyn.

"Or talk all the time," said Mervyn.

"And you have to smile at the camera," said Meg.

"I think it's silly to smile at a camera," said Mary-Mary. "*I* shall smile at the man. Unless I don't like him. Then I shan't smile at all."

"It might be a lady," said Meg.

"I still shan't smile if I don't like her," said Mary-Mary.

Then Miriam, Martyn, Mervyn, and Meg all started saying together, "Mother, Mary-Mary's going to spoil the photograph." "She says she's not going to smile." "Don't

— and she smiled at the ceiling —

let's have it done with her." "Can't she have a snapshot taken in the garden?"

But Mother said, "Don't be silly, all of you. Of course, Mary-Mary will smile. Just leave her alone and I'm sure she'll behave beautifully."

Mary-Mary had just begun planning what awful face she would make in front of the camera, because the others were all so sure she was going to spoil the photograph. But when she heard Mother say she was sure she would behave beautifully she changed her mind.

She began practising her smile instead. She smiled at the floor and she smiled at the ceiling. She smiled at the table, she smiled at the chairs, she smiled at everything she could see. But the more she smiled the queerer it felt, and after a while she didn't feel as if she was smiling at all. It made her face ache. So, just to give her face a rest, she blew out her cheeks and crossed her eyes. Then she tried on the smile again.

'Why are you making such awful faces, Mary-Mary?" said Miriam.

"I'm not," said Mary-Mary, rather surprised. "I'm getting ready to have my photograph taken."

"Oh, dear, I *know* she's going to spoil it!" said Mirian to Mother. "*Can't* we all be done separately?"

And Martyn and Mervyn said, "Yes, do let's."

And Meg said, "Can I have mine in the silver frame?"

But Mother said, "No. I think you're all being very silly. And, in any case, there's a photograph in the silver frame already—one of Miriam and Martyn when they were babies. Now, do leave Mary-Mary alone. She'll be perfectly all right if you don't worry her."

Mary-Mary went out and looked in the hall mirror to see if her smile really looked as funny as it felt. She tried smiling at herself for quite a long time. But the longer she looked at her face in the glass the queerer it looked.

"It's funny," she said to herself. "It's quite easy to smile by mistake, but it's really very difficult to smile on purpose. Perhaps it's because I'm not smiling *at* anyone. I'll try again at dinner-time."

Then, just to give her face a rest, she tried making some interesting new faces that were very ugly indeed.

"They may come in useful next time the others are rude to me," she said to herself.

At dinner-time Miriam said to Mary-Mary, "Why are

– tried making some interesting new faces –

you making that extraordinary face at me?"

"I'm not," said Mary-Mary. "I'm smiling at you."

"Well, don't," said Miriam. "It looks awful."

Mary-Mary made one of her interesting new faces instead, but Miriam pretended not to see.

A little later Mother said, "What's the matter, Mary-Mary, dear? Have you got a tummy ache?"

"No," said Mary-Mary. "I'm smiling at you."

Mother looked surprised. Then she said, "That isn't your ordinary smile, darling. What are you doing it for?"

"I'm practising for the photograph," said Mary-Mary.

"There you are, you see!" said Miriam, Martyn, Mervyn, and Meg, all together. "What did we tell you?" "She is going to spoil it!" "She's practising all these awful faces to make in front of the camera."

Mary-Mary didn't make the rest of her interesting new faces at them, because no one was looking at her. Instead she decided to save them for another time, and went away to find Moppet, her toy mouse.

Moppet was lying under the chest of drawers in the bedroom. Mary-Mary pulled him out, brushed the fluff off his fur, and stared closely into his tiny black eyes.

"Watch carefully, Moppet," she said. Then she smiled at him.

"What did I look like?" asked Mary-Mary.

"Oh, you looked just like a toothpaste lady!" she said in Moppet's voice.

"Good," said Mary-Mary. "I hoped I did."

She went back to the sitting-room, put her head round the door, and said, "*Moppet* says I smile just like a toothpaste lady."

Then, before anyone could answer, she shut the door quickly and went away to play in the garden.

The very next day they all got ready to go to the photographer's. They had their shoes polished, their nails scrubbed, and their hair brushed, and Mother said she had never seen them all looking so clean and neat and tidy all at the same time.

When they got to the photographer's a lady with golden hair smiled at them a great deal, and showed them into a room behind the shop, where there was a thick carpet on the floor and a large camera standing in the corner.

Mary-Mary liked the colour of the lady's hair very much, but she decided to save her smile for when the photograph was taken, in case she couldn't do it twice.

The lady found a chair for Mother in a corner behind the camera; then she looked at all the children, still smiling,

"Now keep just like that, can you?"

and said to Mother, "How would you like them taken—all together or one at a time?"

Mother said, "All together, please. I think I would like them standing in a row."

"Yes," said the lady, "that would make a very nice picture.

So Miriam, Martyn, Mervyn, Meg, and Mary-Mary all stood in a row together, while the lady turned on a very bright light and did things to the camera. She kept smiling all the time as she bobbed up and down this way and that, looking at them from every direction and saying, "Yes, that's lovely. Now keep just like that, can you?"

Then she went behind the camera.

Mary-Mary put on the smile she had been practising so as to be ready for the photograph to be taken. Then she looked out of the corner of her eye to see if the others were smiling too. But Miriam, Martyn, Mervyn, and Meg were all looking at her.

Miriam had her eyes wide open and was shaking her head at her. Martyn was frowning. Mervyn had his mouth screwed up into a round 'O'. And Meg was looking very cross indeed.

Mary-Mary thought they looked so funny, all standing in a row making faces at her without saying a word, that she suddenly laughed out loud.

"All right," said the lady, bobbing about behind the camera. "Now we'll try another one, shall we?"

Everyone looked surprised. Then Mary-Mary said, "Another what?"

"Another picture," said the lady. "I've taken one already, but I think some of you moved. Now, are you all ready?"

Mary-Mary began smiling again, so as to be ready for the next photograph to be taken.

"Tell her to stop making faces," whispered Miriam to Martyn.

"Tell her to stop making faces," whispered Martyn to Mervyn.

"Tell her to stop making faces," whispered Mervyn to Meg.

"Tell her to stop making faces," whispered Meg to Mary-Mary.

Mary-Mary looked at the lady and saw that she was looking at them all with her eyes screwed up and her head on one side.

She turned to Meg and whispered back, "No. You tell her. I don't think she can help it."

~ all standing in a row making faces at her ~

Then Miriam, Martyn, Mervyn, and Meg all whispered at once, "No, *you*. Stop making faces."

"Oh, I thought you meant the lady!" whispered Mary-Mary, and she burst out laughing again.

Then the lady said, "Thank you very much. I think that will do nicely."

After that they all put on their hats and coats, and Mother talked to the lady about when the photographs would be ready and where they were to be sent. Then they all set off home again.

On the way Miriam said to Mother, "I'm sure Mary-Mary spoiled the photograph. She kept making faces and laughing."

But Mother said, "Oh, no, I'm sure it will be lovely. Wait till you see it. I expect we shall all be surprised how nice it is."

A week later there was a loud *rat-tat* on the front door, and the postman handed in a large, stiff envelope, addressed to Mother.

"Oh, it's our photograph!" cried Miriam.

"Can we open it?" said Martyn.

"No, give it to Mother," said Mervyn.

"Let's have a look," said Meg.

"Me too," said Mary-Mary.

And they all crowded round while Mother opened the envelope.

Then everyone said, "Oh!" in a very surprised voice, and Mother started laughing. But all the others just stared at the picture as if they couldn't believe their eyes.

For there, in a row, stood Miriam with her eyes wide open, Martyn frowning, Mervyn with his mouth screwed up into a round 'O', and Meg looking very cross indeed. And they were all staring at Mary-Mary. But Mary-Mary herself, right at the end of the row, was looking just the way people ought to look in photographs, all smiling and jolly.

"Oh, but it's *awful*!" said Miriam.

"I look *terrible,*" said Martyn.

"Look at *me,* then," said Mervyn.

"How *dreadful*!" said Meg.

Mother smiled at the photograph, holding it up in front of her.

"But it's lovely of Mary-Mary," she said. "It's quite the best photograph we've ever had of her. And I've always wanted a proper photograph to show to all my friends."

Then Miriam, Martyn, Mervyn, and Meg all said together, "But you *can't* show people a photograph like that!" "We look awful." "Everyone will laugh at us." "It isn't fair."

"No," said Mother, "I don't think I can. I shall have to cut Mary-Mary off the end, and have you four done again another day."

So that is just what she did. She cut Mary-Mary, all smiling and jolly, off the end of the photograph and found that it just fitted the frame which had the picture of Miriam and Martyn, when they were babies, in it.

"I think we might put that old one in the photograph album now," she said. And she took it out and slipped the new one of Mary-Mary into the frame instead. Then she hid the rest of the photograph in a drawer in the writing-desk, promising she wouldn't show it to anyone but Father. And she took Miriam, Martyn, Mervyn, and Meg to the photographer's again another day.

And after that, whenever Mother's friends came to visit her, they would see two photographs on top of the writing-desk. At one end a photograph of Miriam, Martyn, Mervyn, and Meg all in a row, smiling rather carefully, as if they were afraid of making funny faces; and at the other end, in a silver frame all to herself, a photograph of Mary-Mary looking just the way people ought to look in photographs, all smiling and jolly.

So Mary-Mary didn't spoil the photograph, after all,
and that is the end of the story.

2

Mary-Mary and the Snow Giant

One day Mary-Mary woke up and found that some more snow had fallen in the night. There had been snow for two or three days, but it had all got trampled and dirty. Now there was a new white covering over everything. It looked very pretty.

Mary-Mary decided to go out before breakfast and be the very first person to make footprints in the new snow. She dressed quickly and quietly, put on her coat, and crept downstairs. In the hall she found Father's boots.

"Just the thing," said Mary-Mary to herself. "I shall feel like a proper snow giant in those." And she stepped inside them, shoes and all, and went quietly out into the back garden. And nobody else knew anything about it at all.

At breakfast-time Mary-Mary's big brothers and sisters were all very excited, talking about the new snow.

"Let's divide the lawn into four," said Miriam; "then we can each have our own part. I shall make a snow palace in

*—and nobody else
knew anything about it at all ~*

mine."

"Good idea," said Martyn. "I shall make a big white horse in mine."

"I shall make an igloo and be an Eskimo," said Mervyn.

"And I shall make a snow queen," said Meg.

Mary-Mary said, "I shall do something better than all of those. I shall make a snow giant."

But Miriam said, "No, we can't divide the lawn into five."

And Martyn said, "You messed it all up last time, making snowballs and things."

And Mervyn said, "You go round the edges or play in the front."

And Meg said, "Anyway, there isn't any such thing as a snow giant."

"Oh, yes, there is!" said Mary-Mary.

"Oh, no, there isn't," said all the others.

Mary-Mary looked at them all and said slowly, in her most important grown-up voice, "There's been a snow giant in the garden already this morning."

"Rubbish," they said. "We don't believe it."

"Moppet knows there was a snow giant," said Mary-Mary. "Don't you, Moppet?" Then she squeaked, "Yes," in Moppet's voice.

But the others just said, "Nonsense. Don't take any notice of her." Then they all went off to put on their coats and Wellingtons, and go out in the garden.

Mary-Mary stayed in the kitchen with Mother and helped to put away the spoons and forks. In a minute Martyn came to the back door and said, "Mother, has anyone been in our garden?"

"No," said Mother, "not this morning."

"Not Father even?" said Martyn.

"No," said Mother, "not Father even. He went out early. No one else has been here."

"Only the snow giant," said Mary-Mary.

"Oh, don't be silly," said Martyn, and went out again.

Mary-Mary could hear the others all whispering together outside the back door. "It must have been a burglar!" "Let's find out where he went!" "Don't let Mary-Mary come—she'll spoil it." "We'll track him down."

Then they all went creeping along to the garden again.

Mary-Mary stood on a chair and looked out of the kitchen window. She saw Miriam, Martyn, Mervyn, and Meg all walking in a line round the garden, putting their feet carefully into the big footprints she had left, one after the other, and she began laughing to herself because they looked as if they were playing Follow my Leader.

— putting their feet carefully into the big footprints —

"Why don't you go out and play too?" said Mother. So Mary-Mary went and put on her own coat and Wellingtons.

As she was going out the others all came along to the house again to find Mother. They stood in a row in the doorway, looking very solemn and mysterious.

Then Miriam said, "Mother, we think we ought to tell you—there's been a strange man walking in our garden, and we think he may have been a burglar."

"Good gracious!" said Mother. "How do you know?"

"It wasn't a burglar," said Mary-Mary. "It was the—"

"Be quiet, Mary-Mary," said the others.

"We tracked his footprints in the snow," said Martyn.

"Dearie me!" said Mother. "I wonder who it was."

"It was the snow giant," said Mary-Mary. "Once upon a time there was a huge, great snow giant and he—"

"Oh, be quiet, Mary-Mary," said all the others.

"He had huge great boots on," said Miriam.

("That's what I was going to say," said Mary-Mary.)

"He went into the shed," said Martyn.

("Yes, so did the snow giant," said Mary-Mary.)

"And came out again," said Mervyn.

("So did the snow giant," said Mary-Mary.)

"And walked all the way round the garden," said Meg.

("So did the—")

"BE QUIET, Mary-Mary," they all shouted.

"No," said Mother, "don't shout like that. If Mary-Mary wants to tell us something let her. What is it, Mary-Mary?"

"Well," said Mary-Mary, "once upon a time there was a huge, great snow giant."

"There's no such thing," said Miriam.

"—and he came in the garden early in the morning—"

"Not *our* garden," said Martyn.

"—and he sat down in the middle of the lawn—"

"I don't believe it," said Mervyn.

"—and had snow for breakfast and—"

"Rubbish," said Meg.

"No, don't interrupt," said Mother. "Go on, Mary-Mary."

But Mary-Mary was getting cross at being interrupted so much; so she finished off by saying very quickly and loudly, "—and then four silly great children who thought they knew everything came walking into the garden, and they were all rather cross and grumbly, and all their names began with an M. They were called Mumbling, Muttering, Moaning, and—and Mumps, and when the snow giant saw them all grumbling round the garden he—"

But the others all shouted, "Be quiet, Mary-Mary! Why don't you go and play in the front garden and leave us alone?"

So Mary-Mary said, "All right, I will. I thought you wanted to know, but if you don't want to know I won't tell you." And she walked away with her nose in the air.

The snow in the front was nice and thick, and no one had trodden on it except down the path. Mary-Mary decided to make a real snow giant, just outside the sitting-room window.

"Then they'll have to believe in him," she said, "when they see him looking in at the window."

She began making a big pile of snow under the window, and was still hard at work when the postman came in at the gate.

"Hallo," he said. "What are you making?"

Mary-Mary told him. "Would you like to help?" she asked.

The postman said, no, he was sorry he couldn't help because he'd got work to do. But, all the same, he stopped long enough to show her how to roll some really big snowballs and pile them, one on top of the other, under the window; and soon the snow giant was as high as the window-sill.

"I must be off now," said the postman; "but that's quite a nice start for a snowman."

"Thank you very much," said Mary-Mary. "You have helped me a lot. If I wasn't so busy I'd help you take the letters round."

"That's all right," said the postman. "Any day will do for that. You don't get snow every day." And he went off, laughing.

The next person to come in at the gate was the milk-boy. He whistled when he saw the big pile of snow and said, "What's that going to be—a snowman?"

"A snow giant," said Mary-Mary.

"It wants to be bigger than that, then," said the milk-boy.

"Yes, it does," said Mary-Mary. "Would you like to help make it bigger?"

"What, me?" said the milk-boy. "Oh, no, I've got work to do."

But, all the same, he rolled up his sleeves and set to work to show Mary-Mary how to do it, and in a few minutes the snow giant reached half-way up the window. The milk-boy stepped back, puffing and blowing and wiping his face on a big red handkerchief

"That's going to be a bit of all right," he said. "But I must be off."

"Thank you very much," said Mary-Mary. "You *have* helped me a lot. If I wasn't so busy I'd help you with the milk-bottles."

"That's all right," said the milk-boy. "Any old day will do for that." And he ran off up the road after the milk-cart.

Mary-Mary looked at the snow giant and decided he was tall enough now. All he needed was his head. She wasn't big enough to reach up, not even if she stood on the window-sill; so she decided to make it separately and ask someone else to lift it up when it was finished.

She rolled a very big snowball to the middle of the front gate and patted it smooth. Then she put two pebbles in for eyes, a lump of snow for a nose, and a twig from the hedge

"I'm sorry my snow giant's head is in the way."

to make a mouth. It began to look very jolly. Mary-Mary laughed and put her own woolly cap on top. Then she picked some small green branches from the hedge and stuck them into the snowball all round the edges of the woolly cap. They looked just like hair. Then she made some eyebrows as well, to match.

A van drew up in front of the house, and the laundry-man got down and came to the front gate with a big box under his arm. He grinned at Mary-Mary sitting in the snow by the great big snowball. Then he rested the box on the wall for a moment, and began adding up sums in a little notebook.

"I'm sorry my snow giant's head is in the way," said Mary-Mary.

"That's all right," said the laundry-man. "I expect I can step over it."

"He's got a body over there," said Mary-Mary, pointing to it.

"That's nice," said the laundry-man, still adding up sums.

"I think he'd really rather his head was on his body," said Mary-Mary. "It would be much easier for him than having it kicking around by the gate, wouldn't it?"

"Yes, I expect it would," said the laundry-man, still busy with his notebook.

"It's so much nicer to be all in one piece, don't you think?" said Mary-Mary.

"Yes, much nicer," said the laundry-man.

"So he'd be awfully glad if you'd do it for him," said Mary-Mary.

The laundry-man shut his little book, put his pencil behind his ear, and picked up the laundry box again.

"*If* you would be so kind," said Mary-Mary very politely, and, getting up quickly, she stood in front of the snowball so that the laundry-man couldn't step over it.

"Eh?" said the man. "What do you want me to do?"

"Put his head on for him, please," said Mary-Mary. "He can't do it himself and I'm not tall enough to reach."

"Oh, I see!" said the laundry-man, laughing. "Yes, I'll do it for you. Which way round do you want him?"

"Looking in, please," said Mary-Mary. "I want him to give my big brothers and sisters a very small fright, because they said they didn't believe in him."

The laundry-man looked at the side of the snowball which had the face on it.

"Oh, yes, he's a fine fellow," he said. "I don't think he'll frighten them much. He's got a nice smile."

"Yes, hasn't he?" said Mary-Mary. "I made it. It's a twig really."

The laundry-man lifted the snow giant's head very carefully and put it on top of the snow giant's body in front of the sitting-room window. One of the pebble eyes fell out, and some of the green hair came out from under the woolly cap; but he lifted Mary-Mary up, and she put them back in the right places.

Then Mary-Mary said, "Thank you very much. You *have* helped me a lot. Shall I help you do the laundry to make up?"

But the laundry-man said, no, there was no need, because luckily he didn't have to wash the clothes; he only had to drive the van from house to house to collect the boxes.

When the laundry-man had driven away again, Mother made a hot chocolate drink and called all the children in from the garden.

Miriam, Martyn, Mervyn, and Meg came in, stamping the snow from their boots and blowing on their cold fingers.

"Well, how did you all get on?" said Mother.

"We haven't finished yet," said Miriam. "We spent such a lot of time looking for the burglar."

"There wasn't any burglar," said Mary-Mary.

"How do *you* know?" said the others.

"Because I know who it was," said Mary-Mary.

"Look here—*do* you know anything about it?" said Martyn.

"Of course I do," said Mary-Mary.

"Who was it, then?"

— smiling in at the window —

"I told you," said Mary-Mary. "It was the snow gi—"

"Oh, yes, I know all about your old snow giant," said Martyn. "But who was it really?"

"Me, of course," said Mary-Mary.

"But they were huge, great footprints!" said Miriam.

"I know," said Mary-Mary. "I had Father's boots on. That's why I was being a snow giant, and I *did* sit down in the middle of the lawn and I *did* eat some snow."

"*Well*, you might have told us!" said Martyn.

"Well, really," said Mother. "I do think you're all rather silly. Mary-Mary tried to tell you over and over again, but you just wouldn't listen."

"Yes, but she kept on talking about a snow giant," they said; "and we knew there was no such thing."

"But there *is*," said Mary-Mary, "and if you don't believe me go into the sitting-room and have a look."

"Into the *sitting*-room!" said Mother. "Oh, Mary-Mary, what *have* you been doing? Surely you haven't brought a whole lot of snow into the house! Oh, dear! Oh, dear!"

And she ran along the passage, with the others all following, and opened the door into the sitting-room. Then Mary-Mary heard Mother laughing and laughing, and she heard the others all saying, "Oh, my goodness!" "How did she do it?" "Isn't it huge?" and " I bet some one helped her!"

Then Mary-Mary began laughing too, and ran after them all. And when she saw her snow giant smiling in at the window with his twiggy mouth and his pebble eyes and his green-leaf hair sticking out from under the woolly cap she laughed more than ever, because he really did look so splendid and surprising.

"Well," said Mother, "I think you'll all have to agree that Mary-Mary's snow giant is quite the best thing in the garden!"

And they all had to agree that he was, and Mary-Mary was so pleased with herself that she turned head over heels nine times running, all round the sitting-room floor.

"The trouble with Mary-Mary is she's much too big for her boots," said Martyn.

"Oh, no!" said Mary-Mary, surprised. "The boots were much too big for me."

So there was a snow giant in Mary-Mary's garden, after all, and that is the end of the story.

3

Mary-Mary Finds a Primrose

ONE day Mary-Mary had nothing special to do. So she went all round the house to see what everyone else was doing.

Mother was looking inside a trunk in the box-room.

"What are you looking for?" said Mary-Mary.

"I'm looking for dust-sheets," said Mother. "I need them to cover the furniture to keep it clean while I'm sweeping."

Mary-Mary thought that was rather dull; so she said, "Oh," and went away to find out what Miriam was doing.

Miriam was in the bedroom, looking at her face very hard in the looking-glass. She looked first this way and then that way, squinting down her nose.

"What are you looking for?" said Mary-Mary.

Miriam said crossly, "I'm not looking for anything. I can see it, and it looks awful."

"What does?" said Mary-Mary.

"This spot on my nose," said Miriam. "I must ask Mother

— very gracefully —

what to do about it."

Mary-Mary thought that was rather dull too; so she said, "Oh," and went away to find out what Martyn was doing.

Martyn was scrabbling about in the cupboard under the stairs.

"What are you looking for?" said Mary-Mary.

"I'm looking for a piece of rope," said Martyn. "I want to practise jumping."

"Oh, yes," said Mary-Mary. "I'll jump with you."

"No," said Martyn. "I want to do high-jumping. I'm going to practise for the school sports. You can't jump, but you can watch."

Mary-Mary thought that would be very dull too; so she went away to find out what Mervyn was doing.

Mervyn was searching through the toy cupboard.

'What are you looking for?" said Mary-Mary.

"I'm looking for my motor-boat," said Mervyn. "Now

the ice has melted on the pond I want to mend it so that I can sail it."

Mary-Mary thought it would be dull watching Mervyn look for his boat; so she went away to find out what Meg was doing.

Meg was playing the piano downstairs.

"That's nice," thought Mary-Mary, "I can dance and sing to the music and pretend I'm a theatre lady."

So she opened the door and danced into the room on tiptoe, with her arms spread out very gracefully on either side of her and her eyes closed, so as to look as if she thought the music was very sweet and beautiful. But because her eyes were shut she didn't see where she was going; so she tripped over the hearthrug and fell in the middle of the floor with a big bump.

Meg stopped playing the piano and looked round crossly without saying anything. Then she looked back at the music on the piano and stared at it hard.

Mary-Mary got up and stood ready to dance again, with her skirt held out on each side and her right foot pointed in front of her. But Meg just went on staring hard at the music.

"What are you looking for?" said Mary-Mary.

"I'm looking for the place," said Meg.

"What place?" said Mary-Mary.

"The place I'd got to when you came in and interrupted me," said Meg. "Now, go away. You can see I'm busy, and I've still got to do my scales."

Mary-Mary thought that even a theatre lady would find it rather dull to try to dance to scales; so she went away

- one pretty little pale yellow primrose -

and found Moppet, who was sitting on her pillow, looking over the top of the eiderdown with bright beady black eyes.

"Everyone seems to be looking for something," said Mary-Mary to Moppet. "We'd better go and look for something too."

"What shall we look for?" she asked in Moppet's tiny, squeaky voice.

"Anything," said Mary-Mary. "It doesn't matter what. If we don't know what we're looking for we might find something really nice."

So she carried Moppet downstairs and out into the garden. They walked all the way round the garden, but couldn't see anything special at all; so then Mary-Mary said in Moppet's voice, "Don't let's look for anything big; let's look for something very, very small—about my size."

"All right," she said. And she put Moppet in her pocket and crawled along the flower-bed on her hands and knees, trying to make herself as small as Moppet.

And that was how she found the primrose.

It was growing all by itself, half hidden under dead leaves, one pretty little pale-yellow primrose.

"I do believe it's the only flower in the garden," said Mary-Mary. "And *I* found it! I must go and tell the others."

She found Mother in the sitting-room, covering the tables and chairs with white dust-sheets. Mary-Mary ran in and said, "Mother, guess what I've found!"

But Mother said, "Not now, darling. Run away, there's a good girl. I'm busy this morning." And she climbed up on top of a ladder and started dusting the picture-rail.

Mary-Mary crawled under a little table and began to play tents. She pulled the sheet this way and that, trying to make a nice opening for her tent, and then, because she pulled too hard, the whole table fell over on its side with a clatter and Mary-Mary was quite covered up in the dust-sheet.

Mother looked down from the top of the ladder and said, "Now, Mary-Mary, you really must run away. This isn't a game. This is spring cleaning."

So Mary-Mary climbed out from under the dust-sheet and went away to tell someone else about her primrose.

She found Miriam still in the bedroom looking in the looking-glass and putting white cream on her nose.

"Miriam," said Mary-Mary, "shall I tell you what I've just found?"

"No," said Miriam, "not now. You can see I'm busy."

Mary-Mary went up to the dressing-table and looked at the cream jar.

"That's fun," she said. "You look like a circus clown. I'll be a clown too." And she put her fingers in the cream jar.

Miriam grabbed it from her. "No, not you," she said. "You don't need cream on. What you need is a good wash.

Whamm!

You're all covered in earth."

"Why do you need it, then?" said Mary-Mary.

"Because of this spot on my nose," said Miriam. "Mother says it's the spring. Now, do go *away*, Mary-Mary."

So Mary-Mary went away to find Martyn. He had fixed up a rope in the dining-room. One end was tied to the table-leg, and the other end hung over the door-handle. Mary-Mary opened the door just as Martyn was going to jump over the rope.

"Guess what I've found, Martyn!" said Mary-Mary.

"Oh, bother!" said Martyn. "Why must you come and interrupt me? Now, do be quiet. You can stay and watch if you like, but don't talk."

So Mary-Mary went in and sat in the big armchair and watched Martyn. But she soon got tired of this; so she climbed up on to the back of the big chair and began jumping down into the seat every time Martyn jumped over the rope.

"Suddenly there was a loud *whamm*!

"What was that?" said Mary-Mary.

"You naughty girl," said Martyn. "That was the spring."

"What do you mean?" said Mary-Mary.

"The spring of the chair," said Martyn. "It sounds as if you've broken it by jumping on it. You'd better go away quickly before you break anything else."

So Mary-Mary went away to find Mervyn (because she still hadn't told anybody about her primrose). Mervyn was sitting on the floor by the toy cupboard with his motor-boat on his knee.

"Guess what I've found!" said Mary-Mary.

"No, not now," said Mervyn. "I'm busy trying to mend this."

"What's the matter with it?" said Mary-Mary.

"I think the spring's broken," said Mervyn.

Mary-Mary didn't want to hear any more about broken springs; so she went away to find Meg.

Meg was still playing the piano. Mary-Mary went and stood beside her, waiting for her to finish so that she could tell her about the primrose. But Meg didn't finish. She went on and on, playing the same notes over and over again, and playing them wrong nearly every time. Mary-Mary thought it was a very loud and lumpy sort of piece, and wondered what it could be called.

Soon she grew tired of waiting for Meg to stop playing; so she began playing herself, very softly, on the low notes.

"Stop it," said Meg, still playing hard.

So Mary-Mary went round to the other side and began playing very softly on the high notes.

"Go *away*," said Meg, and stopped playing.

"Would you like to hear what I've found?" said Mary-Mary.

"No, I wouldn't," said Meg. "Can't you see I'm practising?"

"What are you practising for?" said Mary-Mary.

"For the school concert," said Meg. "And it's jolly hard."

"It sounds it," said Mary-Mary. "Is it about a giant? Or is it elephants playing ball?"

"Don't be silly," said Meg. "It's called Spring Song. Now do go *away* and stop bothering."

So Mary-Mary did go away; and, because there was no one else to tell about the primrose, she went out of the front door and down the front path, and started swinging on the front gate. It was warm and sunny, and some birds in the tree close by were chirping and twittering loudly.

Mr Bassett came along the road, whistling to himself. He smiled when he saw Mary-Mary, and said, "Hallo."

"Hallo," said Mary-Mary. "Why are you whistling?"

"Because it's such a lovely day," said Mr Bassett. "Spring is coming, Mary-Mary."

"I know," said Mary-Mary. "It's come already in our house."

"How do you mean?" said Mr Bassett.

"Well," said Mary-Mary, "Mother's spring-cleaning, and Miriam's got a spot on her nose (and she says that's the spring), and I jumped on a chair and it made a funny noise (and Martyn said *that* was the spring, too), and Mervyn's putting a new spring in his motor-boat, and Meg's playing a piece like elephants dancing on the piano (and she said *that* was a Spring Song), so I think we've got a lot more spring than we need in our house."

"Oh, dear," said Mr Bassett, "I didn't mean spring-cleaning and things like that. I was thinking about the birds all nesting in the trees, and the ice being melted on the pond, and the spring flowers that will soon be coming up in the garden."

Then Mary-Mary said, "Guess what I've found!"

And Mr Bassett said, "A crocus?"

And Mary-Mary said, "No. A primrose."

And Mr Bassett said, "Well, that really *is* a bit of spring! They must all be coming up in Bramley Woods too."

"The others are all too busy to come and see my primrose," said Mary-Mary; "so they don't know about it yet."

"Then you'll have to take it to them," said Mr Bassett.

So Mary-Mary went and picked her primrose, and, as she hadn't got a vase, she put it in a jam-jar filled with water. Then, when it was dinner-time, while Mother was fetching the plates in from the kitchen, Mary-Mary put the primrose in the jar on the table in front of Mother's place.

"Whatever's that?" said Miriam.

"One flower," said Martyn.

"In a great big jam-jar," said Mervyn.

"It looks silly all by itself," said Meg.

Then they all said together, "Don't put it there, Mary-Mary." "Mother won't have room to put the plates

"I think you're all jolly silly."

down." "You're spilling the water on the cloth." "The jar's too big for it."

Then Mary-Mary suddenly began shouting out in a loud, cross voice, "I think you're all jolly silly. If you weren't so cross and busy and beastly, bothering about spring-cleaning and spring spots and broken chair-springs and motor-boat springs and lumpy old Spring Songs on the piano you might have found this primrose yourselves, and *then* you might have remembered that it was really spring."

Just then Mother came in with the plates, and when she saw the primrose in the jam-jar she said, "Oh, it's a lovely little primrose! The first I've seen this year. Who found it?"

But Mary-Mary was still talking to the others (though she wasn't shouting quite so loudly now) "—and if one primrose can grow in our garden," she said, "when everyone's cross and busy and beastly and not bothering about it at all, then there must be hundreds and *hundreds* of primroses growing in Bramley Woods where nobody's cross and busy and beastly. And if *I* were a mother with a whole lot of cross and busy and beastly children I'd go to Bramley Woods and have a picnic there and pick primroses!"

Then Miriam and Martyn and Mervyn and Meg all started talking at once. But Mother said, "No, hush. Mary-Mary is quite right. I think we really had forgotten it was spring, and I'd quite forgotten about the primroses in Bramley Woods. They must be lovely there just now. Shall we do as Mary-Mary says and all have a picnic?

Then everyone said, "Oh, yes!" "Hooray!" "A picnic!" "How clever of Mary-Mary to have thought of it!"

And Mother said, "Yes, it shall be Mary-Mary's own picnic, because she is the only person who remembered it was really spring!

So they all went for a picnic to Bramley Woods because Mary-Mary had found the very first primrose, and that is the end of the story.

4

Mary-Mary and Miss Muffin

ONE day Mary-Mary was bored. All her big brothers and sisters were reading or writing or drawing or knitting, but Mary-Mary was doing nothing.

She tried talking to them, she tried jumping up and down in front of them, she tried making faces at them; but all they said was, "Oh, stop bothering, Mary-Mary!"

So Mary-Mary stopped bothering. Instead, she said in a dreamy voice, "I think it's time Miss Muffin came again."

When Mary-Mary said this everybody groaned, because they knew what it meant.

It meant that Mary-Mary, dressed in some of Mother's old clothes, was going to come knocking at the front door, saying she was Miss Muffin and had come to tea. Then everyone had to be polite to her and ask her in and treat her as if she were a real visitor. If they didn't Miss Muffin made such a scene, marching up and down in front of the gate and shouting that "some people had no manners",

"I think it's time Miss Muffin came again."

that they were all ashamed of her and had to hurry out and bring her indoors before a crowd collected.

The first time Mary-Mary had come knocking on the door, saying she was Miss Muffin, it had been a great success. Father had been at home, and he had invited her in most politely and never shown that he guessed it might really be Mary-Mary. And when the others had started to say, "Don't be silly—we know who you are really," Father had looked quite shocked and said, "Hush! It's all right for you to be rude to each other or to Mary-Mary; but Miss Muffin is a visitor and must be treated politely."

Mary-Mary had loved this, of course, and Miriam, Martyn, Mervyn, and Meg were afraid she would want to be

Miss Muffin every day. But Father had said, quite definitely, as he was showing her out of the door, "Good-bye, Miss Muffin. It *has* been nice having you. We shall look forward to your coming again, *but that won't be for a long while, of course.*"

Mary-Mary had started to say, "Oh, but I could come again tomorrow. . ."

But Father had put his finger on his lips and said, "No—not if you are really Miss Muffin, because Miss Muffin is a lady, and ladies know that they can't come to tea very often without being invited."

"Yes, of course," said Mary-Mary in Miss Muffin's voice. "I shall only come very sometimes, not at all very often. Thank you for such a nice afternoon. Your children have been most polite to me."

For a while Mary-Mary had been quite good about only being Miss Muffin sometimes and not very often. But soon she took to being Miss Muffin oftener and oftener, and once Miss Muffin had even invited herself to tea two days running. Miriam, Martyn, Mervyn, and Meg had shut the door in her face, and it was then that Miss Muffin had made the dreadful scene outside the front gate.

So today, when Mary-Mary said, "I think it's time Miss Muffin came again," everybody groaned.

Then Mother said quickly, "No, I can't do with any visitors to-day—I'm too busy. Miss Muffin must come another day."

"When?" said Mary-Mary. "Tomorrow?"

"Perhaps," said Mother. "It all depends how busy I am. No, not tomorrow. It's the Garden Fête. I must bake some cakes to take along there."

The Garden Fête was going to be held two afternoons running at the house of a lady called Miss Stokes. She had a large garden, and if the weather was fine the stalls and the teas were going to be out of doors.

"Can we go to the Garden Fête too?" said Miriam.

"Yes," said Mother. "We will all go tomorrow."

"Oh, *why* not today?" said Miriam, Martyn, Mervyn, and Meg all together.

"I told you why," said Mother. "But now I come to think of it, there's really no reason why you shouldn't go by yourselves."

Miriam, Martyn, Mervyn, and Meg were all very pleased.

"But do we have to take Mary-Mary?" they said.

"No. You four go on your own today," said Mother. "I'll take Mary-Mary tomorrow."

Then she gave them threepence each to get in (because it was half-price for children) and ninepence each to spend there.

Mary-Mary stood at the gate and watched them go. They felt rather sorry for her when they saw her standing there.

"Never mind," they said. "Perhaps Miss Muffin can come another day."

"Yes, perhaps she can," said Mary-Mary, "and perhaps she can't. And perhaps she can come today and perhaps she can't. It all depends how busy she is."

They looked rather surprised at this. Then Miriam said, "Come on, she's only pretending. Let's go." And they all said, "Never mind, Mary-Mary," again, and waved good-bye to her all the way down the road.

Mary-Mary went on thinking rather hard about Miss Muffin.

"Perhaps she can and perhaps she can't," she said out loud, to nobody in particular. "It all depends how busy she is. I'd better find out."

Then she dialled a pretend telephone number on the gate, pulled a branch of the hedge close to her ear, and said very fast, in an important, grown-up voice, "*Ting-a-ling, ting-a-ling.* Hallo, Miss Muffn—is that you? Are you busy today? No, I'm bored to death. Oh, good. Well, there's a garden fête at Miss Stokes' house. Oh, hooray—thank you for telling me. I could just do with a garden fête. I've never been to one before. No, I thought you hadn't. Good-bye."

"Well, that settles that," said Mary-Mary. "Miss Muffin *is* coming today. I *thought* she was."

She ran quickly upstairs, pulled out a box from under her bed, and took out Miss Muffin's old, battered hat and purple-flowered dress. Then she ran downstairs again and put them on in front of the hall mirror, nodding at herself and talking to herself all the time.

In the kitchen she could hear Mother getting out the baking-tins, then someone knocking at the back door, then Mrs Merry's voice saying she'd just popped in as she was passing.

"That's lucky," said Mary-Mary, putting on the old, battered hat. "Mrs Merry's just popped in, so I'll just pop out. When Mrs Merry pops in she doesn't pop out again for ages and ages; so if I pop out now no one'll miss me. But just in *case* they do, I'll pop a note in the letter-box saying I've popped out; then I'll pop off."

"That sounded rather good," said Mary-Mary. "I wish I could remember how I did it."

Then she wrote a note saying, "Dear Mrs Madam, Just popped out to the Fate. Yours truly, Miss, Muffin," and popped it in the letter-box.

Last of all she ran out and dug up her dreadful old handbag out of the sandpit. She had to keep it there when she wasn't using it because it was so very old and dreadful-looking that people always wanted to throw it away when they saw it lying around. It had belonged to Mother a very long while ago.

She opened it to see what was inside. There were only two buttons, an elastic band, and an empty cigarette packet.

"Never mind," said Miss Muffin. "Money isn't everything." And she closed it with a snap and set off to the Garden Fête.

She ran all the way there, holding up her skirt so as not to trip over it. On the fence outside Miss Stokes' house was a large notice which she stopped to read. It said:

COME TO THE GARDEN FETE—STALLS,
SIDESHOWS, AND STRAWBERRY TEAS
PLEASE WALK IN

"Thank you, I will," said Miss Muffin, and she straightened her hat and walked in.

At the top of the drive a lady was sitting at a little table

– a large notice which she stopped to read.

taking money from the people who were coming in (sixpence for grown-ups and half-price for children). Miss Muffin bent down low, picked up her skirt, and ran as fast as she could right past the little table, and through a rose arch into the garden. The lady at the table looked up quickly.

"Who was that funny little person?" she said.

But nobody seemed to know.

"Oh, well, I expect she was something to do with one of the sideshows," said the lady, and went on taking the sixpences.

Miriam, Martyn, Mervyn, and Meg each spent their ninepence at the Garden Fête. First they spent threepence each on an ice-cream (but that didn't last long). Then they spent threepence each on the hoop-la stall (but none of

"Who was that funny little person?"

them won anything). Then they spent threepence each on the lucky dip.

Miriam won two marbles.

"What ever do I want with those?" she said.

Martyn won a doll's knife and fork.

"That's no use to me," he said.

Mervyn won a pink plastic hair-slide, but didn't even feel funny enough to put it on. And Meg won a box of pistol caps.

"I should call that an unlucky dip," said Martyn. "I'd rather have had another ice-cream."

"So would I," said the others. Then they all said together, "Never mind—we'll save them for Mary-Mary."

After that they stood in a group near the tea garden, sadly watching the people having strawberry teas at the little tables and wishing they had saved their ice-creams till now instead of buying them right at the beginning.

Just as they were wondering whether to go home the four Merry children came by. Barbara, Billy, Bunty, and Bob were all laughing and looking very jolly.

"I say!" said Barbara to Miriam. "Have you seen who's at the White Elephant stall?"

"The *what*?" said Miriam. "Surely they haven't got elephants here?"

"No, of course not. 'White elephants' just means anything you don't want and don't know how to get rid of. People bring them to fêtes, and then sometimes other people buy them." She began laughing again; so did the others.

"Well, what's so funny about that?" said Miriam, who was beginning to want her tea quite a lot.

"It isn't funny at all," said Martyn, who was hungry. "I don't see anything to laugh at," said Mervyn, who was thirsty.

"Nor do I," said Meg, who was tired.

"You will if you go to the White Elephant stall," said the Merrys, and they all went off, laughing.

Just then Miss Stokes came hurrying out of the tea garden.

"Hallo! How are you all?" she said. "And how is your dear mother? I haven't seen her for such a long time. And how is your baby brother, or is it a sister?"

"We have a little sister," said Miriam.

"But she's not quite a baby any more," said Martyn.

"She's at home with Mother," said Mervyn.

"They're coming tomorrow," said Meg.

"Well, that *is* nice," said Miss Stokes. "I shall look forward to seeing them both. And now you must come and see my stall—it's the White Elephant stall and I've been doing so well. I've got a wonderful helper."

She led them down to the far end of the garden, where they saw quite a little crowd collected round one of the stalls. As they came nearer they heard people laughing. Then all of a sudden Martyn said, " Look who's there!"

They all looked, and high up above the people's heads, standing on the stall itself, what should they see but a funny little person, no bigger than Mary-Mary, in a battered old hat and a purple-flowered dress.

"Why, it's Mm—!" Miriam was just going to say 'Mary-Mary,' but Miss Stokes said, "Miss Muffin, that's right. It's little Miss Muffin. Do you know her?"

"Well, sort of," mumbled Miriam, Martyn, Mervyn, and Meg. "We have seen her before."

"That's nice," said Miss Stokes; "then you must come and meet her. She's been *such* a success. I've sold nearly everything off my stall since she started helping me. Such a funny little thing—she told me her name was Muffin, but I don't know any family of that name. I was a bit worried at first—she seemed so small to be here alone; but she said she'd just popped in as she was passing, and she had some big brothers and sisters here. So I supposed it was all right, and she's been *such* a success on the stall."

Miss Stokes pushed her way through the crowd with the others following. It was quite difficult to get near the stall, because so many people were coming away with their arms full of things: old lampshades, picture-frames, china ornaments, and all sorts of odds and ends. One man was even wheeling an old pram full of odd-sized dinner plates, old hats, and saucepans.

"What should I do with those?" said a man in the front —

"Yes," said Miss Stokes in a whisper, "they've all been bought at the White Elephant stall!"

They pushed their way nearer and saw that Miss Muffin, on top of the stall, was waving a large bunch of paper flowers.

"Only threepence!" she was calling out in a high, squeaky voice. "Who'll buy a big bunch of flowers for threepence?"

"What should I do with those?" said a man in the front.

"You could put one in your buttonhole, and give the rest to your lady," said Miss Muffin. "And here's a jug, a very

113

nice jug. Who'd like to buy this jug?" She picked up a large white bedroom jug that was standing in a basin beside her.

"What's it for?" said the man down in front.

Miss Muffin looked at it. "Well, it's a bit big for milk," she said, "but you could use it for a vase. The handle makes it easier to fill." She put the bunch of paper flowers in it. "There you are," she said, "if you buy both together they're very pretty."

"But what about the basin?" said the man.

"Oh, that's for sailing boats in, if you're a man, or making puddings in, if you're a lady. It's a very useful basin—you can use it for both."

"But I haven't got a boat," said the man, smiling, "and my lady has a pudding basin already. What should I do with it?"

Miss Muffin thought hard, then she said brightly, "I know—you could wash in it!"

Every one laughed because that was what the basin was really for; then the man said, "All right, you win," and he handed up the money for all three.

He took one of the paper flowers and put it in his buttonhole, then he handed the rest of the bunch back to Miss Muffin.

"Keep those for yourself," he said. Then off he went, carrying the big china jug and basin.

"Oh, goody!" said Miss Stokes. "I never thought we'd get rid of those." Then she pushed her way to the front.

"Miss Muffin," she called, "here are some friends of yours. Would you like to come down now and see them? You've done so well I've hardly anything left to sell; so if you'd like to take your friends to tea I'll give you the tickets."

So Miss Muffin was lifted down from the stall, and Miss Stokes thanked her very much indeed for her valuable help, and brought out a long strip of pink paper, which was five tea tickets all joined together.

"Take those to the tea garden," she said, "and you and your friends will just be in nice time for the strawberry teas."

So Miriam, Martyn, Mervyn, and Meg all sat at a table under a large striped umbrella with Miss Muffin, and had strawberries and bread and butter and jam, and little iced cakes as well.

"You see," said Mary-Mary, nodding at them under the large battered hat and wiping her sticky fingers on the purple-flowered dress, "Miss Muffin is quite a useful person to know sometimes. You ought to be polite to her *every* time she comes."

So Mary-Mary and her big brothers and sisters all had strawberry teas at the Garden Fête, thanks to Miss Muffin, and that is the end of the story.

5

Mary-Mary Makes
the Morning Exciting

ONE Saturday morning Mary-Mary's mother was out, and Mary-Mary's big brothers and sisters were all feeling rather dull. They wandered about the house and in and out of the garden, saying, "What shall we do? How *boring* everything is! I wish something interesting would happen."

"What sort of interesting?" said Mary-Mary, who was blowing air into a paper bag.

"Oh, anything," said Miriam.

"Some men coming to dig up the road," said Martyn.

"Or the fire engine coming," said Mervyn.

"Or someone cutting a tree down," said Meg.

Mary-Mary screwed up the top of the bag, then clapped her hands on it so that it burst with a loud pop. Then she said, "If *I* wanted something interesting to happen I'd make it happen," and she stumped off upstairs.

A few minutes later Miriam, Martyn, Mervyn, and Meg heard a great thumping and bumping noise going on overhead. They all ran out into the hall and shouted up the stairs, "What ever are you doing, Mary-Mary?"

"Something exciting," said Mary-Mary.

"Well, stop it," they said.

"You won't say that when you see me come floating down the stairs," said Mary-Mary.

"What ever do you mean?" said Miriam.

"I'm learning to fly," said Mary-Mary.

"It sounds as if you're jumping off the bed," said Miriam.

"Oh, no, I'm *flying* off the bed," said Mary-Mary. "Like Peter Pan."

"Well, don't," said Miriam. "The ceiling will fall down."

"Well, that would be exciting too," said Mary-Mary.

"Don't be silly," said Miriam, Martyn, Mervyn, and Meg all together, and they went back into the sitting-room.

Mary-Mary stopped trying to fly, and instead she fetched Moppet from the top of the toy cupboard and whispered in his ear, "You and I will go and do something exciting all by ourselves. We'll play shipwrecks in the bath."

She fetched her little sailing-boat and carried it into the bathroom with Moppet. Then she filled the bath with water, put Moppet in the little boat, and floated him out to sea in the middle of the bath.

Moppet floated round quite nicely in the little boat for a while, then Mary-Mary said, "Look out, sailor—there's a storm coming up in a minute!" And she took the bath-brush and stirred up the water into little waves, so that the boat rocked up and down, just as if it were in a rough sea.

Some of the water splashed over the edge of the bath and made Mary-Mary's feet wet, so she took off her shoes and socks. Then she locked the bathroom door.

"I will hide the key in a safe and secret place," she said to Moppet, "because it would be a pity if someone came in while the sea was rough and interrupted *me* just as I was going to save you."

Then, when she had hidden the key, she stirred up some more waves with the bath-brush, and slowly the little boat filled with water and began to sink.

"Save me!" she squeaked in Moppet's voice.

"Yes," said Mary-Mary in a beautiful, dreamy voice. "I am a mermaid and I will save you."

She reached down into the water and pulled Moppet out just before the little boat sank to the bottom. Then she sat on the edge of the bath, at the tap end, with Moppet in her lap.

"Oh, thank you, thank you!" she squeaked. "You have saved my life. Tell me who you are."

"I am a mermaid," sang Mary-Mary in the beautiful dreamy voice, "and I am sitting on a rock in the middle of the sea, combing my beautiful long hair." And, as she had no comb, she brushed her hair with the big bath-brush until it stood out in short, wet spikes all round her head.

"I have a beautiful palace at the bottom of the sea, all made of shells," she sang, "and you shall come there with me and be my mermouse, and we will live happily ever after."

Then she let the plug out, and when the water had run away she and Moppet climbed in and sat in the bottom of

"– in the middle of the sea, combing my beautiful long hair –"

the bath and had a large pretend feast of fish and shrimps in the mermaid's palace.

But the bottom of the bath was cold and wet. So after a while Mary-Mary said to Moppet, "I'm getting rather tired of living happily ever after, aren't you? Let's get out and be ordinary people again." And they climbed out of the bath and went to open the door. But the door of the bathroom was locked.

Mary-Mary rattled the handle; then she remembered.

"Of course," she said. "I locked it myself. And I hid the key in a safe and secret place. Now, I wonder where that could have been? Oh, yes—I expect it was under the bath."

But it wasn't. Mary-Mary looked all round the bathroom, under the bath, in the laundry box, and on the window-sill; but she couldn't find the key anywhere.

"It *must* have been a safe and secret place if I can't even

— but she couldn't find the key anywhere —

find it myself," she said.

Then she heard the others calling to her. "Where are you, Mary-Mary?"

"I'm here," said Mary-Mary.

"Come down at once," said Miriam.

"I can't," said Mary-Mary.

"Why not?" said Martyn.

"I can't unlock the door," said Mary-Mary.

"Oh, goodness!" said Meg. "Now what are we going to do?"

They all stood outside the door and rattled the handle and talked and shouted and banged on the door, but still Mary-Mary was shut up inside.

"Can't you really remember where you put the key?" said Miriam.

"No, truly I can't," said Mary-Mary. And she truly

couldn't. "Perhaps it's gone down the plug-hole," she said.

"Oh, you silly girl," said Miriam, Martyn, Mervyn, and Meg all together, and they all went on talking and arguing about how they should get her out.

Miriam went to ask Miss Summers next door if she could help, but Miss Summers was out. Then Meg went to ask Mr Bassett, who lived near by; but he was out too.

Mary-Mary began to get tired of being shut up in the bathroom.

"I'm getting hungry," she said.

"Oh, goodness!" said Meg, outside the door. "Will she starve?"

"Of course she won't," said Mervyn.

"But we ought to get her out, all the same," said Martyn.

"What ever shall we do?" said Miriam.

They whispered and talked outside the door for a bit longer. Then all of a sudden Martyn said, "I know! We could get the fire brigade."

"But why?" said the others. "There isn't a fire."

"No," said Martyn, "but they have long ladders and things. I believe that's what people do when they get stuck in places: they ask the firemen to come and get them out."

"Yes, of course," said Miriam. "Why didn't I think of it before? We'd better go and telephone them."

Then Mary-Mary heard them all running away downstairs.

She forgot to feel hungry any more and began to feel rather excited, looking forward to the firemen coming. But what a pity it would be, she thought, if she should miss seeing the fire engine drive up to the house.

— the big red fire engine —

"If only I could find the key I could get out and watch them arrive," she said to herself. "Anyway, I may as well get all ready just in case I find it."

So she tidied up the bathroom and put on her socks, and then, when she went to put on her shoe, out fell the key on to the floor!

"Of course!" said Mary-Mary. "Now I remember. I put it in my shoe on purpose so that I could forget where it was if anyone came up suddenly and told me to open the door."

When Miriam, Martyn, Mervyn, and Meg had finished telephoning they all went on to the front step to wait for the fire brigade.

In a very short while they heard the clanging of a bell, and a moment later the big red fire engine came roaring up the road and stopped at the front gate. Then four firemen, in helmets and big black boots, jumped quickly down and

"It was ordered specially for me."

ran one after the other up the front path to the house. It was a splendid sight.

Miriam explained all about how her poor little sister had been locked up in the bathroom for hours, and Mother was out, and they hadn't known what to do.

"That's all right," said the biggest fireman. "Don't you worry. We'll have her out in no time."

Then the four firemen went tramping up the stairs in their big black boots, with Miriam, Martyn, Mervyn, and Meg all following behind and telling them which way to go.

But when they got to the landing they all stopped and stared at each other, and the four children said, "Oh!" and the four firemen said, "What's the meaning of this? Have you children been playing a joke on us?" For the bathroom door was wide open and there was no Mary-Mary to be seen!

"No, truly she was here!" they cried. "She was locked

in, and we didn't know what to do. Oh, where ever can she be?" And they all ran from room to room calling her.

Then one of the firemen opened the front bedroom window, and they all looked down into the garden, and there what should they see but Mary-Mary standing by the gate with a whole crowd of people.

The four Merry children were there, and Tommy from up the road, and Stanley, the grocer's boy, with his bicycle, and quite a few grown-ups as well. And Mary-Mary was waving her hand at the fire engine, just as if she owned it, and saying, "Yes, it is nice, isn't it? It was ordered specially for me on the telephone."

"But where's the fire?" said Stanley, the grocer's boy.

"There isn't one," said Mary-Mary. "Don't be silly. We didn't want a fire; we only wanted a fire engine."

"Ooh, you are lucky!" said Tommy from up the road. "I wish the fire engine would come to our house."

Just then Miriam and the others saw Mother hurrying up the road with her shopping-basket on her arm. They all ran downstairs as fast as they could to meet her.

"It's all right," they cried, "there isn't a fire!" Then they told her all about what had happened.

"Thank goodness for that!" said Mother, and she hurried indoors and told the firemen how sorry she was, and how the children had really thought they were doing the right thing. Then she made them all a cup of tea.

The firemen were very nice and said accidents did happen sometimes, and they were glad the children hadn't been playing a joke on them, because that would be a very serious matter. Then every one suddenly remembered that Mary-Mary was still outside the front gate. So Mother sent Miriam to fetch her in.

Mary-Mary came in with her wet hair still sticking out in spikes all round her head, and her hands and knees black where she had climbed up on the wall to watch the fire engine arrive. Her face was black too, where she had rubbed it with her hands.

"I know now what I'm going to be when I grow up," she said, smiling brightly at them all. "I'm going to be a fire lady."

"So you're the young lady who was locked up in the coal cellar?" said one of the firemen.

"Oh, no," said Mary-Mary. "I was locked up in the bathroom."

"Were you really, now?" said the fireman. "I wonder what made me think it was the coal cellar."

Mary-Mary couldn't think either; but, as everybody laughed, she laughed too. It was fun having four real firemen drinking tea in her house on a Saturday morning.

When they had finished their tea the firemen showed Miriam, Martyn, Mervyn, and Meg all sorts of interesting things: the ladders with hooks on them for climbing up the walls of houses; the hoses, coiled up tightly like Swiss rolls, that could be joined together to make one long one if they wanted it; and even the little iron lid that covered the hole in the road where they got the water to put out a fire.

Then they all said good-bye, and thank you for the tea, and thank you for coming; and Miriam, Martyn, Mervyn,

Meg, and Mary-Mary waved until the fire engine was out of sight.

"Well, that *was* fun!" said Miriam.

"Just what we wanted!" said Martyn.

"Better than having the road dug up," said Mervyn.

"Or a tree cut down," said Meg.

"I'm so glad you liked it," said Mary-Mary, smiling proudly at them all.

"Good gracious, Mary-Mary!" they said. "Do you mean to say you did all that on purpose?"

"No, not quite," said Mary-Mary. "I really did lose the key. But when I found it again I thought how disappointed you'd all be, because I knew you so specially wanted something interesting to happen. And I couldn't dig up the road for you, or cut a tree down, but I'd jolly nearly got you a fire engine without meaning to, so I ran away and hid because I thought it would be such a pity to spoil it."

"That *was* sweet of you," said Miriam.

"You *are* a sport," said Martyn.

"Thanks *awfully*, Mary-Mary," said Mervyn.

"But you'd better not do it again," said Meg.

"Oh, no," said Mary-Mary, "once is enough. But I am glad you all enjoyed it."

So Mary-Mary made the morning exciting, after all, and that is the end of the story.

JOAN G. ROBINSON

Joan G. Robinson (1910–88) was the second of four children to barrister parents. She trained as an illustrator and in 1939 began writing and illustrating stories for the very young. She published over thirty books in her lifetime for three different age groups. In 1953 the first of her enduringly popular *Teddy Robinson* series about her daughter Deborah and her teddy was published, followed by the *Mary-Mary* series, about the youngest of five children. In 1967 *When Marnie Was There* was shortlisted for the Carnegie Medal.